Prais

The meticulousl
When We Were H
edge-of-the-grid ....xico where the
postal service won't go, but UPS will," but the seasonally-
employed fringes of society and the secret corners of the
human heart. Michel-Cassidy is a smart, sly yet compas-
sionate observer of how her people do their jobs, how they
talk—what an ear!—and how they manage to take care of
themselves and each other.

David Gates, author of *A Hand Reached Down to Guide Me* and *Jernigan*

From slopeside to seaside, mountains to mesa, Linda Michel-
Cassidy takes us to "off-the-map" places, into the heart of
the risky, hardscrabble, troubled yet wonder-struck lives her
people are making there. What do we humans need to survive and, more than that, figure out what we're here for?
Sometimes these seekers get a magical rush of excitement,
"like [they] were on the verge of something new." That's how
I feel as I read Michel-Cassidy's stunning short stories. I'm
left caring deeply about what the future might hold for these
unforgettable characters, and their creator. "Everything is
epic," proclaims one of her pitch-perfect narrators. *When We
Were Hardcore* is an epic debut collection.

Ellen Lesser, author of *The Shoplifter's Apprentice* and *The Blue Streak*

EASTOVER
— PRESS —

When We Were Hardcore is an accomplished and moving collection. Linda Michel-Cassidy has a gift for locating those moments that shift the trajectory of a life, highlighting those fragile ties to family and home.

Jill McCorkle, author of *Old Crimes* and *Hieroglyphics*

When We Were Hardcore reveals characters of the American West that we've never seen, they possess the curiosity and bravado to test its wildness and the endurance and grace to receive its beauty. Linda Michel-Cassidy's debut is a knock-out. These stories unfurl with a steady honesty and sly humor beneath, across a landscape that never promises more than what's held in this moment. They show us what it means to be human in nature.

Kelly Sather, author of *Small in Real Life*

WHEN

WE

WERE

HARDCORE

⟨ ⟩

Linda Michel-Cassidy

When We Were Hardcore

Linda Michel-Cassidy

ISBN   978-1-958094-50-1

FICTION

BOOK DESIGN ◊ EK Larken
COVER ART ◊ Linda Michel-Cassidy
AUTHOR PHOTO ◊ Jia Oak Baker

PUBLISHED IN THE UNITED STATES OF AMERICA BY

EASTOVER
— PRESS —

Rochester, Massachusetts
www.EastOverPress.com

WHEN

WE

WERE

HARDCORE

⟨◊⟩

Finding a fitting place for oneself in the world is finding a place for oneself in a story.

—Jo Carson,
AS QUOTED BY LUCY LIPPARD IN *THE LURE OF THE LOCAL*

⟨◊⟩

CONTENTS

As Happy as I Could Remember

Hawk found the house, out on the mesa, where a bunch of people could stay cheap by just doing repairs. It was solar, which was the right thing for us. Marley knew of the place, said it was straw bale. I had a hard time picturing what that would be like, made of hay. You'd have thought it would blow away and all, three-little-pigs-style. Marley told me it was round, like a yurt or a kiva, words which sounded ancient. I was picturing an igloo, except brown, because of the mud, which is what holds the straw down.

"You know, if they're not done right, those bale houses can have bugs, big-time," Marley said. "Critters, too. And mold." We were at the pay-what-you-can café, where I'd first met everyone. The planning felt exciting, like we were on the verge of something new.

"A little discomfort might be good for you," Hawk added. "Maybe it's time for you to experience the pain of the working class." Hawk tapped the metal straw on his bowl of maté which, now that I remember, he hadn't paid for. I'd be sure to remember this moment, the map Hawk drew on a napkin, basically an "X" for where we were, and a long squiggly line ending I don't know where.

Marley was actually from here, all his life. He was born in one of the communes, from back when. But then his dad wandered off and his mom fell in with a bunch of Gaia women and ended up in Sedona. He was left on his own to bump around town. I'm not sure why he wasn't in school. Marley said nobody bothers with kids like him unless they get arrested, and Hawk said something about life *is* school, which even I know is a little on the nutty side.

After finishing my first ridiculous year of college, before Marley and Hawk came into my life, I road-tripped into the desert with my cousin, Hattie.

"We need an adventure," she'd said, pointing to the Grand Canyon on a crumpled map. It was a ten-year-old one we'd gotten from the free bin, but we were sure something that big still had to be there.

"If you say so," I said. What else was I going to do, what with my mom's new husband skulking around the house all day? I'd figured I'd best be out of there before my grades came in.

As soon as we hit Santa Fe, Hattie met some guy, in the tire store of all places. I was like, *No way, Hattie— you promised we could head north.* As I dragged her back to the car, the mutt slipped her a note. He had on a big old hat and unscuffed boots. I told her I didn't think he was an actual cowboy, but as she said, I was no authority on realness. Our worries soon enough became not hitting tumbleweeds and wondering if coyotes go after humans. We saw fifteen deer and one loose cow before we even made the next county.

We landed in this sketchy hostel where everyone smelled like patchouli. This was right before we were supposed to head back. *To the real world*, my stepdad would have said. I needed to make the school-or-no-school decision, and quick.

"What's the point?" this crazy-tall old guy said, busting in on our conversation. "Pay money to The Man and then go work for him?" This was Hawk. I thought he made a good argument. Hattie didn't see it, but she was looking to ditch me anyway, to go see that guy back down in Santa Fe.

"I'll be back in a week," she'd said, leaving me there at the hostel, all alone.

"Fine," I said, as if I had a choice. "I like it better here anyway." A person knows when they're extra baggage. It would have been nice if she'd left me the car.

Hawk, Marley, and this other woman with them, Lilly, had gone out to the hostel trying to find out some clues. After Lilly's younger brother had gone missing, the cops hadn't taken her report seriously. So some young guy from away comes here and then he's gone. *We'll let you know, honey,* they'd said, pretty much telling her that her brother, Joe, was just another wandering loser.

"He's still here," she said. "I just know it. I feel it." I believed her, because I liked her the moment I met her, the way her every smile was also a grimace. Whatever she wanted, I wanted for her. When she sat down, she reached back and swept her braids over her shoulders so she didn't sit on them. Her hair was so long that I pictured it growing out since she was my

13

age, ten years of hair, maybe fifteen? It was hard to tell. I heard somewhere that the hair shows trauma, the way the rings in tree trunks do. As she told me about Joe, she played with the splitty, sun-bleached ends like they were worry beads. She made him sound like he was part of a fable. "He has such a full soul, but he's sort of different," she said. "Too gentle, too inward. People think he's not paying attention or that he's stupid, but he has a very busy mind." She had come here in the spring to check up on him. He'd been hanging with some crazy people, *whacked*-crazy, so she'd tried to get him to go back home with her, maybe pressing too hard. Then he vanished.

It was in those first few days, that in-between of being a visitor and when you start to sink into a place, that I got to know Hawk, then Lilly and Marley. This new life of mine, this fresh way of being, was some sort of a rebirth for me—that's what Hawk said. Maybe I didn't entirely choose to be marooned here, but also it could be destiny—the world confirming what Hawk said. Marley made a slow and wide smile and bobbed his head, so mellow. Lilly looked at me like she was thinking of something else entirely, kind of the way she described Joe, but of course I didn't say that. They were the opposite of everyone I knew before.

I just tumbled on in with them. I mean, I had to be somewhere, right? Why not go with the folks who seemed to actually want me around? The mystery and sadness about Joe had lashed them together. I was just a subset. Or a placeholder. Still, it was something.

I was so untethered—and yet, the spot we'd settled in felt solid. Weighty. I loved how basic my sleeping pallet was, wood frame, low on the floor. It made me feel like one of those religions where they live all stripped down and simple. "All a person needs," Hawk said the first time we came out here, "is a place for rest." It wasn't even in a room—the building had no inside walls—which weirded me out at first. You get used to things. You block out noises, learn to make fewer sounds. You begin to forget about the dust that is everywhere, or simply become part of it.

You got out to the house by a long, rutted dirt road that was a wash. It didn't even have a name, just a yellow paint mark on a post. During monsoon season, when the ground is dry and hard and those rains come so quickly, it becomes a river. Around the house was a wall made of old tires and glass bottles all held together by more mud. I'd seen pictures of this sort of thing, but that's never the same. When the sunlight flashed the ends of the bottles, it made it look like a present.

The first time I went, Hattie long-gone, Hawk showed me around like he was telling me a secret. "Voila!" he said. Inside were the pallets with straw-filled mattresses, maybe eight of them, and a little kitchen area. The bathroom was any place not in the house.

We were way, way out on the mesa, beyond the mobile homes and some fancy off-grid houses, past an old school bus that had its seats taken out to make room for a bed and a couch. At first it felt all flat, brown, and dusty, but after a while, you learn to pay attention. A little pink bud on a cactus or an orange stripe on a spider—it's all there—you just have to look a little closer. People said that there were some of those survivalists out that way with hoards of rifles and a couple of wives each, but I really never saw anything like that. Any time anyone pulled out a gun, it had been about a rattlesnake.

The open space had me freaked at first. All that

15

horizon! I hadn't expected it to be so huge. Because there is so little out in the desert, you can't tell the size of anything, including yourself. Things may be shrunken or puffed up gigantically, and you'd never know. When the sun is setting, I swear you can see the curve of the earth, like you could run toward it and disappear over the crest.

The place where they all lived back when Joe was here didn't even have the pallets. They'd taken over an abandoned herder's shack made of wood scrubbed smooth by the brutal winters. Added some lean-to, some old rice sacks for curtains. There was a fireplace and an horno outside for making bread, but no stove. They did things authentically, over a fire, truly by hand. No one had a car, at least for a while, and they made the fifteen-mile trip to town by hitchhiking.

"It was a different era," Hawk said.

"It was mayhem," Lilly said.

"Peyote," Marley said into my ear.

Lilly said Joe wouldn't have gone, at least not by choice, and left his dog, Mr. Tim Buckley, behind. He and that dog were too in love with each other for Joe to have left him just sitting there, waiting. Before, he had taken the husky pup on when he was off exploring the Southwest. His having Mr. Tim would have made it harder to catch a ride, but he kept him along anyhow. We all loved Mr. Tim being around, but also, every time he'd come in close for an ear rub was a reminder that Joe *wasn't* here.

Joe had first made his move to the mesa with only a backpack and a bedroll. "He was just a cliché," Lilly said. I didn't believe she thought so little of him or else she wouldn't have come for him and stayed on trying to find out what happened. Their father said drugs. But Lilly said she never thought that. "He had—*has*—this sadness in him. Always did, even as a kid." She said that like she had lived a life already, but she couldn't have been more than a decade or so older than me. There was something spent about her, though. She told me that usually it's either people running from here as fast as they can, or people running from something else *to* here. "Of course, Marley has nowhere else to go," she said. This was a thing I'd thought about myself—not that Hattie didn't also have a hand in it.

According to Hawk and this woman, Juniper, who happened by every now and then to scream at Hawk, one day Joe was here and the next day, not.

"Out into the mesa," Hawk said.

"Off the bridge," said everyone else.

"People don't just disappear," I'd added, hoping what I said was the right thing for Lilly but also worrying for Hattie. And myself. I was lost. Not in a places-on-a-map way, but in a what-am-I-on-this-earth-for way. Hawk told me that what we needed was to work together and to eschew—*eschew!* He used that exact word. I wrote it down. So smart! He read everything. Sometimes, he'd flip through a dictionary and point out the things the authors got wrong. Anyhow, we were to eschew stuff that's commercial, those things that you buy. And that sure made sense, what with people thinking a solid bank balance will make everything right, like that's all it comes down to. *Honey, it will be fine, you'll grow to like him. Be happy for me, just a little.* She actually said that, out loud, my mom did.

Every two-three days, I'd go down to the hostel and see if Hattie had turned up. I made Xeroxed signs of a photo booth picture of us we'd taken at a diner on Route 66 that was shaped like a massive covered wagon. I circled her with a red marker and added *Have You Seen Me?* as if she were a parakeet I'd accidentally let out. I tacked them up in the expected places: the grocery, the hostel, and the coffee shop. I hadn't even gotten the name of that guy she knew in Santa Fe, and to be honest, I hadn't cared that much. "Hattie *was* the one that split, after all," said Lilly, when I told her how I landed here. She summoned the right amount of anger towards Hattie—one more reason I felt mothered by Lilly.

And I thought Lilly liked having left-behind people around, like it might cancel out the disappointment of her not mattering enough if there were a cluster of us.

Sometimes in the mornings, forgetting for a minute where I was, I'd be startled awake by this feeling that there wasn't enough gravity. I was falling in love with the never-endingness of this place. It felt reliable. I could count on the wind barreling through like an out-of-control train and that I'd see a rainbow after nearly every storm. You can look at a cliff out this way and know that the dinosaurs were here and that it looked pretty much the same now as it did then.

I wrote letters back home to my mother. I was on the fifth I'd written—the fifth I'd rip up. I didn't want to send mail and not get any back. Plus, I'd have to either lie or account for misplacing Hattie. But going through the writing of them, even if they never got sent, felt like good practice for the explaining I'd have to do eventually. Still, you'd think someone from my family, Hattie, or my mom, anybody, would make some kind of an effort to come for me. To try and find me.

So here I was. New family, living in a new way. For me, at least. Things felt very earthbound, maybe even historic, here in our us-made home. I imagined things would be fine. Better than fine.

One afternoon, I was resting on the mattress I was supposed to be stuffing, kind of a futon filled with a whole bunch of different things: hay, wool, ripped-up fabric. Marley nudged me with the top of his head. "Hey there, Space-out." This was a thing that he did when I was off in a daze, gently head-butting me awake, his dreads swinging, like brushes in a car wash, but dry. "House meetup," he said, rolling his eyes. We'd usually just air a bunch of feelings, talk a few things out, do the group hug, and then get on with what needed getting done.

"What about? Food? Water? Bad attitudes?"

"Nope," Marley said. "Heat."

Hawk said that to winter here was a test: if you could stick until spring, you were golden. I was scared of the deep cold but also sort of charged up by thinking about it. What it could be like to be snowbound, whether the snow would block out the daylight. How close we'd have to huddle to share our warmth, happy for Mr. Tim's hot breath in our faces. Whether my ribs would show. I'd seen pictures of caved-in roofs, damage from the winds. I saw that Hawk had raised a dare. If I made it through until spring, I wondered if that would mean this was where I lived.

Once the days got short and the frost set in, we were chopping wood like crazy. Marley and Hawk went up into the mountains and cut piñon, and Lilly and I stacked it under the eaves of the house. We had three piles as tall as I could reach. Hawk wanted to sell off some of the wood, but we voted to wait and see if there even was extra. I'd heard that some years you plowed through the wood just trying to stay warm, and then there was too much snow to go for more. That's when people start burning their furniture. Of course, to do that you had to have had some to begin with.

I'd scored a job, temporary, but still, running the Christmas tree stand from the lot at the gas station. The guy who drove the mesa kids in on the school bus—those that went—gave me a lift in. Going home and on the weekend, I'd hitch. Two bucks for every tree I sold. And tips. Probably because of being a girl, sure, gender-based and all, but you know what? I folded those dollar bills right up and put them away in the little embroidered bag I wore under my shirt. Lilly said the guy who hired me didn't have a cut permit and that I'd better not get caught. Sometimes no one came for hours, so I just sat under the scratchy churro blankets that the guy who brought the trees gave me and read books I had borrowed from the hostel. *Trout Fishing in America, Zen and the Art of Motorcycle Maintenance, Howl*. I was trying to catch up. When I'd leave for the night, having counted the money and thrown a tarp over the trees no one bought, it was getting down in the 20s, or so said the light-up sign at the bank across the road.

After a couple weeks of me selling trees, Lilly announced a Girls' Day Out: half work and half not. We collected our change and went to the laundromat— this was the work part. Our clothes would ice up if we hung them outside, and if we dried them in the house, they'd end up smelling like all of us plus smoke. We were yapping about going to the burrito truck for a treat when Lilly all of a sudden screamed and went after this guy at the dryer.

"Those clothes," she said. She was vibrating, she was so shocked. "Give them to me. They're Joe's. GET your hands off!" The poor guy ran out, arms full of jeans and shirts. He looked freaked, but Lilly can do that to a person. She stood behind his car blocking him in, pounding on the trunk. He said he'd found them, and threw some back at her, then screeched out of the lot. Lilly's knees buckled, and she crumpled onto the curb. I'd never heard someone wail like that. I called the cops from the payphone inside, but the lady there at dispatch said it didn't sound like any kind of emergency to her.

Right there, next to the phone, was one of the posters I'd put up about Hattie. No one had ripped off any of the strips with the hostel's number on it. I never got any messages about her. I'd seen the posters around town, right where I left them, yellowed and curled, until they got covered up by someone else's eight-and-a-half-by-eleven-inch version of a problem.

The day before winter solstice, Lilly, Marley, me, and Hawk bombed up the drive in his truck, me in the back with the neck of my shirt pulled up to my nose to keep the dust out of my teeth. A gorgeous sunset. Sky-blue-pink, Lilly called it. We all loved each other right then. I was feeling that I was a part of them, at least more than I was of anyone else.

"Yeah, man! Solstice eve!" Marley said. It was a production around here, bigger than Day of the Dead.

"We need a bonfire," Hawk said, too charged up to consider that we'd be using up January's heat.

"Bonfire without me," I said. I was having a hard time getting used to cold being a regular thing, plus I was always exhausted, from hustling the Christmas trees and standing around waiting to catch a ride back out to the mesa.

I fell right asleep and was half-woken by tickling. I thought it was Marley, come to bug me, but everyone was outside. They were going on about how much wood we could spare for the bonfire—we couldn't go and burn it up in one brilliant night. Something brushed me, just a feathering, but it was there: a flash of fur. I screamed and swung my feet around. The floor was so chilly, just cement. Mr. Tim ran in, smelling of campfire, and launched himself onto me.

"What is it, honey? Are you hurt?" Lilly said, rushing in, breathless. I told her, and she laughed. "If a mouse is all that's bothering you, then maybe save your screaming for something real."

I wanted to wash my feet, like with bleach or something, but we had this whole water thing going on. We hauled it in, using big plastic tubs. We had no water of our own, but no one out on the mesa did. "Use it sparingly, one bath a week," Hawk said. Still, we ran out. Leave the lid off those containers for an hour in the desert and it's all gone. Sometimes we got it at the rest stop at The Gorge lookout, where tourists line themselves up against the metal rail to take pictures of each other, the bridge over the Rio Grande as the background. It's wonderful to see, there's no denying it. Sure, it's a big old crack in the earth, but it's something beyond that. Visitors with their sunburnt noses and brand-new cowboy hats would stare at us saying, *I didn't think there were hippies anymore.* Usually, we were so in the moment that we didn't pay them any notice. I'd just look around and think how beautiful everyone was and how lucky I was that this was my world.

Still. Those mice! I had seen mouse poop in the cabinets where we kept the onions and nuts and such but had told myself that it was just crumbs or seeds.

We had cats for that sort of thing. "They're full of fleas," Lilly said, "Do not let them in." They're feral, and a lot of them are orange. The little ones were cute in their kitten ways, but the grown ones would scratch your eyes out. They wandered around the outside of the house, birthing and birthing again. "Coyotes get most of the babies," Lilly said. "Otherwise, there'd be hundreds of them." When you hear the coyotes howling and yipping, calling each other in to dine, it's really hard to not picture those fuzzy kitten heads with their tiny pink tongues.

Hattie finally sent me a postcard, care of the hostel. I went down there to change up some of my tip money into laundry quarters and to see if anyone there wanted to come to our solstice ceremony. The postmark was from Las Vegas and had a picture of those white tigers. She wrote that she wished I was there, but that's just a thing that people write when they have nothing else to say. It wasn't like I could write her back or get there or anything. I used it as a bookmark, for a while. By that time, she could have been anywhere, including back here, which she wasn't.

Sometimes, as I tried to go to sleep, I'd think that I could freeze into a popsicle during the night and never know. In the morning, I'd have to find the wool socks and hat I wore to bed, but later kicked off, before I could even think about getting up. Mr. Tim had adopted me, so he slept on my pallet, which was perfect, because he threw off warmth. He followed me all over now, like I was his new Joe. He seemed to know when I felt overwhelmed. Sometimes, in the morning, he was clutching my hat like it was his stuffie.

Solstice morning, but still the middle of the night, I was in a half-awake, but still-dreaming blur, the kind where there is a chance to be able to drift back to sleep. Lilly was all, "Wake up! It's time." Right in my ear. If it had been light outside, I'd have seen our breaths—it was that cold. Everyone but me was already moving into the day, including Mr. Tim.

"Get up! Now, or we're going without you," Hawk said. "It's a magical day." It's the tradition to go out to The Gorge to celebrate, which seemed somewhat bogus, since the worst weather was ahead of us. People bring a vegetable or something else they'd grown or made and offer it up. I'm not sure who the asking was aimed at, but I hoped ours would be about Joe. The plan was to be way out by a particular spot before the sun came up. We gathered up half-frozen water bottles, blankets, dried fruit, bread, and such. Like the pioneers!

The truck had been left running to warm, and its lights silhouetted Hawk and Marley hustling to get ready. In the fog of exhaust, they looked like a special effect. Mr. Tim, seeing the truck running—that dog sure loved a ride—jumped in the back, skittered to the front of the bed, settling in on some potato sacks and old blankets.

"Ready?" Hawk said to me. "I'm so excited for you. Your first solstice!" Like I was about to get an award.

I pictured a circle, and they were all inside of it—lit up—and there's me, running around the outside, looking for a way in.

I huddled in the bed of the truck with Mr. Tim. The road bumped along under us, right in my spine. I hummed and heard myself warble inside of my ears. It was a new-moon night with more stars than my eyes could handle. Something about it being so cold made them seem sharper and closer. *A starry canopy*, that's something Lilly said. In school they don't tell you that there are this many of them, or maybe they do, but it's a number in a textbook. You memorize the shapes, The Big Dipper, Ursa Minor, but doing that tells you nothing about how stars really are. That sky was something I couldn't have learned without being there in that truck, shivering my way through the longest night of the winter.

At moments like this, I'd imagine Joe was here, with us. On the ride out to The Gorge, he, Mr. Tim, and I would sit in the back of the truck, cupping our mittens over our ears to keep the wind out. He'd hum a song that felt familiar but that I couldn't place.

Marley slid open the little window between the cab and the bed and said, "Ready for the show?" When Hawk turned off the headlights, we flew down the road unlit. More and more pinpricks of light were over us, and I then knew why the sky had to be so wide. I was as happy as I could remember being in a long time, maybe ever.

We rattled into the parking lot where people leave their cars when they go on hikes along The Gorge in summer. They walk along the Rio Grande and look out over the rift saying: *Water did this. Imagine.* They're wrong, of course: volcanoes and earthquakes did it—even I know that. But who wants to be next to an 800-foot hole and be thinking about earthquakes? Often, they don't expect how thirsty they'll get, taking pictures of each other, kicking a stone over the edge and waiting to see if they can hear it plonk into the river. They return to their parboiled cars, a rage of a headache parched into their skulls. They find their candy bars have melted, tubes of sunblock splooged all over the seats, and sometimes the pets they stupidly left behind—just for a moment—are dead. I've heard that they dare to wait until no one is around and carry their heat-struck poodles to the edge, tossing their curly-haired bodies into the crevice. This rafting guide we knew, Tonio, said he saw a tiny dog corpse come flying over the edge, hurling into the water right in front of his raft, splashing a tourist lady who was sitting up front. But Tonio said a lot of things.

A few vehicles were parked in the lot. Marley said they were probably just some folks car-camping, but it was hard to imagine wanting to do that, this time of year. It was like a moonwalk. In the parking lot, under the glaring lamps, the night sky seemed dark. But just a few yards out, the moon took over. The landscape was crisp, and welcoming, and huge. And for once, I felt a part of it, and whole with my found family, and not at all a shadow of anyone else. "This special place," Lilly said. "I feel he's here." Our plan was to go about a half mile to a clearing that in good weather is a picnic spot. I'd heard there were all kinds of hoodoo out there. I was ready.

Way back when, they'd have to cross the river by going down into The Gorge and up again, with mules and carts. Plenty of people didn't get to the other side. Came all that way and never made it. Imagine.

Hawk had assured me that the energy out there would blow my mind, that this was one of the most powerful days of the year. "We can share in it and be reinvigorated," he said. Sometimes he reminded me of a wizard. Before, I had only known solstice as a date I needed to memorize for an astronomy class, which I took because there was no dissection and it was supposed to be easy, which it was not. We did learn why it was the longest night of the year, something about the sun being so far south. The magic part was never mentioned.

Mr. Tim, who had been quietly following behind us, took off after a rustle in the weeds. Lilly crooked her arm through mine. She came out here a lot. To think, to collect sage for making the smudge sticks that she sold outside the grocery, but mostly to see if she could sense anything of her brother. She told me that lately she'd been feeling his spirit was out here, calling her to find him. She said it made her happy because maybe he was better off now.

The sun began to peek up, the sky lightening to greyish-yellow where it met the scrubby horizon. There were some people further along, outlined by a bonfire. There were a lot of them, swaying, chanting in low tones. They were scary and fantastic at the same time. If only they'd been a mirage.

"Fucking witches," Hawk said. He dropped the supplies and put his arms out, his palms back as if to keep us from danger.

"Oh, no," Lilly said, like she knew something not so spiritual was about to happen.

Mr. Tim Buckley, probably not expecting either the negative energy or the extra people, started running in circles and barking.

I wanted to leave, so those women could go on with whatever sorcery they were up to. The singing or spellcasting or whatever it was seemed like something out of a movie that Hattie and I would have made fun of. Being next to it was just creepy.

"Relax," Lilly said. "No one's going to put a curse

on you. It's just the Wiccans. They come out of the woodwork this time of the year. They're just a bunch of yoga instructors and realtors."

Up close, they did look like regular people, but in black and purple floaty clothes. They sort of reminded me of Lilly, just more so, like how she'll be in the future. Not that I would have said this to her. There were a lot of women like that in town: hair grown long, allowed to go gray, their bodies relaxed and fleshy. There was something mothery about it, not at all scary. Hawk was staring straight at them, his jaw clenched.

"Goddamn weirdo svengali," Lilly would say when Hawk said things that were sounding too mystical or when he assigned her work that she felt was gender-based, like washing his clothes. But at that moment he looked like a regular old, angry guy who needed a haircut and a shave.

"Hawk, man, let's just go somewhere else," Marley said. "Find us another spot." They were still a ways from us, like several truck lengths, but out here with no one else around, any extra people feel too close, especially if they're going to cast a spell on you.

Once, when I was out this way filling the water drums, I heard a guy with a Texas accent and creased jeans say, "This is just the kind of place you could go to hide. You could come here, kill your wife, and no one would know."

"You bastard!" one of the purplest women said. She made a move in our direction, but two of the other witches grabbed her sausagy arm. One spoke into her ear. She shrugged them off, running at Hawk. "Where's my child support, you scum!" she screamed. Mister Tim growled at her. Another one, who I'd seen at the co-op where you buy dried beans in paper bags—I remembered her because she had this hand-sized tattoo of a triangle on her sternum with an eye in the middle looking right at you—she picked up a fistful of pebbles and threw them at him. Those women sure could move. Fabric flapped all around as they swarmed at Hawk, making them look like some kind of demented dance performance.

Hawk just stood there. Not like this hysteria wasn't a surprise, but like it didn't matter.

At the clearing, a kiddie pool-sized circle was marked off with rocks like giant smooth eggs that someone must have hauled up from the river. In the middle of it sat a toddler dressed in a dirty snowsuit. He waved his arms at Mr. Tim. Lilly, Marley, and I crept towards the baby as the chaos continued off to the side.

"Hawk did a pretty good job leaving his spawn all over the Southwest," Lilly said. While Hawk was sort of a father figure, even I could see that, the way he got us all a place to stay and made sure we had some sort of food always—even if it was Lilly that had to cook it in the end—there's no way I could picture him as an actual parent. I guess I didn't really know how a father should operate, but I was pretty sure Hawk wasn't it.

Mr. Tim crept towards the little boy, who reached out his arms and wiggled his fingers. My heart was pounding like crazy, but I wasn't sure if it was because of the incredible energy about the circle and that kid sitting there or what. Things were getting very intense and not at all mystical or uplifting.

We sat down on our packs and waited. The sun coming up was nice, but it was hard to get into the moment with all that yapping going on. Every so often one of the women would poke at Hawk with a many-ringed finger. That little kid just sat there playing with some pebbles and seemed to know not to put them into his mouth. I watched him anyway, though he was not looking at anyone in particular.

No one had done anything to celebrate the turn of the season. We'd been dreaming of salvation, while convincing ourselves that we had found it. This morning was just like any other, and we were just regular people with—except for Lilly—ordinary problems.

Mr. Tim kicked up the dust as he chased another rabbit he'd never catch. How the coyotes could get them was a mystery to me. Catching the kittens, this I could imagine, since they were so crazy friendly before their wildness set in, they probably walked right up to the coyotes, presenting their fat bellies.

Some of the women returned to their circle of rocks, and I could tell that the day had lost its energy for them as well. Even the ones that still fussed at Hawk were mellowing. Nobody picked up that little kid. The rabbit flew in front of us with Mr. Tim barreling right behind, so close that I felt the air move in a wave.

"He might actually catch it," Marley said. As much as Mr. Tim was my friend, I was rooting for the rabbit. It ducked behind a cluster of sage, and Mr. Tim stopped so short that he rolled. It was natural selection, how a rabbit out here would need to be dirt-colored and so, so fast. But what a human needed to survive, I had yet to figure out.

Lilly was stuck here, or rather, she could not allow herself to be freed. Not even after Tonio would find "the evidence," this being what the police would call what little was left of Joe. They'd put the remains—*male, Caucasian, early to mid-twenties*—in a heavy plastic bag to be floated in Tonio's raft, to be met downstream by the coroner. Lilly would stay, insisting that something of Joe was still there.

Even so, a person can't be selling Christmas trees forever.

I'd get a new job at the sandwich shop and teach the tourists how to pronounce *relleno*. I'd get a knot of muscle in my arm from wrestling with the portafilter on the espresso machine, which is different from the muscles you get dragging Christmas trees or rolling massive barrels of water.

I still had my Christmas tree tip money, more than enough for a Greyhound ticket, if only I knew where to go. Before heading out, I'd hitch to The Gorge, and look down at the Rio Grande one last time. I'd stand on the bridge and feel the rumbling as the trucks passed, running the pad of my index finger along the plaque mounted on the guardrail that describes the depth and breadth of the rift.

WHEN WE WERE HARDCORE

With all the time spent thinking about bears, the giant hump in the backyard shouldn't have come as such a shock. I told myself it was just dirt, that someone had backed up a truck and dumped a massive load of dark, loamy soil right outside of the bedroom slider—but the mound had eyes, beady little black ones. He was both fabulous and terrifying. I shifted my head, as did the bear. The thing about a bear is that seeing it and not seeing it both have their merits.

I tiptoed to the kitchen, like the way they do in cartoons. "Hey come look," I said to the husband. "A bear is here. In our yard." We crept back to the bedroom. "He doesn't look starved, does he?" I asked.

"What's the business with the ears?" the husband said. "Are these the good ones?"

"I'm not sure it matters," I said. "Keep the dogs in."

"I'll grab the camera."

The bear huffed.

I recognized that noise from the other night and remembered his stink. I'd been in the driveway, my arms loaded with work stuff and groceries, when I heard the snuffle coming from a nearby hedge. And that smell, all hot and garbagy! I could never outrun something with an exhale like that. I torqued my intuition, convincing myself that it was the wind, that I'd never heard a thing. I hadn't told the husband, unsure of how to describe such a sensation.

The first time I saw a bear that wasn't a zoo-bear I was on a hike with the dogs. He was just sitting there, eating from a mess of apples. The sun hit the fur on his back and glowed. It wasn't the rustish brown of a cow or the chocolate of a horse, but this other color, like milky cocoa with a wash of charcoal. Supposedly, the black bears are the ones you want to worry about. Something about their ears being different than those of the brown bears. Or maybe it's the other way around. The picture I took on my phone made him look like a heap of soil.

We weren't so entirely rural. We could see wilderness off in the distance, where the power lines stop and the off-gridders live. We were in that ten-mile swath where the postal service won't go, but UPS will. No paved roads, but we could see our neighbors, hear them even. Sound travels well over flat, hard dirt.

Hearing the neighbors was but one of my gripes about our move-out-of-the-city thing. There were these kids next door, always there, constantly making noise. When asked about their being in the yard in the middle of the day, they reported that they were homeschooled. Their parents came and went at regular work hours and didn't appear to be hippies or born-again, so we had questions.

"They have a dish," the husband said. "So what's with the homeschooling?"

They had a very long driveway that ran parallel to ours, like a détente: we're heading in the same direction, but let's keep our distance. A large and scrubby hedge, more like a tangle of sticks, ran between the two roads in, and those kids hid out in that strip of land. When they weren't doing that, they were picking the fruit—apples, plums, peaches—from the trees in our yard and then trying to sell it back to us from a stand they set up at the end of their drive. When all of the low fruit disappeared overnight, I assumed it was the barbarian entrepreneurs.

On the other side of us was a little mobile home, and in it lived an ancient woman with a knotty bun of grey hair. She stayed hidden, except to hang wash or press tortilla dough on a table set on the porch for when the day was too damn hot. Some youngish men came by on summer weekends, yelling, "Hola, Abuela!" They mended the roof and enclosed her porch with green corrugated plastic, making it look like a potting shed. The old woman sat on her stoop nodding at them, cracking beans into her apron. Those men would deposit bags of groceries on her porch and stack another cord of wood, but always head out before dark. It was easy to forget about that tiny lady with her skinny legs poking out of rain boots.

In fact, I only thought of her when a friend from the city visited and stood in my yard, unable to see anything but the trailer. "You should buy that land and ship her out," she'd said.

"People don't do that here," I'd said.

"Everyone has their price."

"Maybe not everyone," I said.

This friend said that she herself could never get any work done with her sense of aesthetics so disturbed. We had a fight about it, the kind of argument that already rests inside of the body, waiting for a portal. She chafed over the slowness of our internet and suffered further agitation because the restaurants closed down at eight o'clock (*if* you can call them that, said she). So, there came a fissure between us, and the only time I remembered about the trailer was when I wondered about the city friend, and soon, I recalled the city friend only when I saw a peek of the green plastic walls as I turned into the driveway. But the way in was quite long, certainly longer than my thoughts of the old woman.

After a cooling interlude, I sent the city friend a bag of roasted piñon. In turn, she sent me fancy pears in little sweaters from Harry and David, but UPS left the box on my porch, where it was reduced to slobber and pulverized cardboard.

The massive animal plopped himself right between the hot tub and our crumbling retaining wall, and there he napped, acquiring a light dusting of snow. I watched him breathing in, breathing out, my own rhythm synchronizing to his. We'd been having sporadic frosts interrupted by blasts of heat, and the mountain animals, confused, had started heading down the hill, frantic to stuff themselves. His fur was mottled, but I didn't know if this meant he was aged or if it was the winter thickness growing in, like it did on our dogs. His tongue slipped out of his long snout every now and then, which, when captured in a photo, made the bear seem almost cute.

There'd been all manner of bear advice going on: Make yourself big. Yell at the bear. Don't leave bags of warm tamales in your car. And not so much advice as a warning: *Do not call Fish and Game or they'll come and shoot it. Right in front of your kids.* It had already happened. The week before, a bear had turned up splashing around in the fountain of a fancy-for-here resort, the kind locals work at but don't go to. Fish and Game tried to tranquilize him and totally missed. Startled the poor bear as well as the mud-wrapped tourists listening to calming music in their private rooms. They shot him right there in the middle of the Talavera-tiled courtyard, the crack of the gun reverberating off the authentic leaded-glass windows. He was just a cub.

The bear eyed the rotten apples that had accumulated under one of our trees. He was definitely brown, but, in all of the excitement, I couldn't remember if that was the scary color or if it was the black. Our tiny dog barked and barked, which set off our other, usually more sensible, dog. The visitor moved towards a tree. I'd call it lumbering, not because he moved slowly, which he did not, but because of his size. Three, maybe four hundred pounds, but know that my bear-measuring experience was limited to never. Think of two and a half generously sized humans. He maneuvered himself rather fast up that tree. A tree not at all built for bears, branches snapping all the way. Then he had another nap. He was wonderful, like having your own wildlife exhibit—a super-scary one that no one would believe existed.

Once or twice, when I'd been sitting at my desk, lining up my pens and remembering what it was like to not have to drive twenty-five miles to get to a real grocery store, I imagined coming home to a broken-in door, the husband gone. Furniture squashed, cereal boxes munched into oblivion, but nothing too messy. Maybe a shoe left behind with a little blood on it. Questions left open-ended, but not. I would tell myself I felt awful for thinking this. Just horrid. But then sometimes, I couldn't help myself. I'd consider what it would be like to call my mother-in-law, to say it was a total surprise—A bear! I'd mail her the shoe, of course, absolutely. "Who could have imagined," I'd say, and she'd agree.

Later, when I'd almost-but-not-really stopped thinking about the bear, came all this yelling, but it was just the everyday screams from those urchins next door. Despite the never-ending mayhem, they did not deserve to be eaten. "Drive over to the neighbors'," I said to the husband. "Those kids should be kept inside." The dogs were whining like maniacs. "Take your phone. I'll call you if he moves."

When the husband returned from next door, I asked what they said, what, if anything, we should do.

"I told the dad there was a bear in our yard and he just said, 'Cool.'"

Eventually, the bear made his way down the tree and resettled somewhere else, maybe into that tumbleweed of a hedge where the truants play, perhaps to wait for us to put out our yummy garbage. He reappeared several hours later and was again harassed by our dogs. He retreated, went up a tree that was closer to the house with the kids but still in our yard. It was an odd kind of relief that he was back. If he was in the tree, then he couldn't be outside of the front door smelling the dinner cooking or at the living room window counting our pets.

"Do we tell the muttonhead next door?" the husband asked.

"I don't know. He should be able to see him up there," I said. "How can you *not* see a many-hundred-pound mass of fur?"

We considered the cub that had gotten shot at the resort and decided that we didn't want to draw any attention to him. No one wants *that* on their hands.

"Let's just see what he does," I said. I recalled a time when a dilemma like this would have sprung from a party game. Which would you chose: backyard bear, or stuck on a desert island with only a mime and a Twister set?

"If he heads their way, we'll let them know," the husband said.

We couldn't let the dogs out, so eventually we hustled them to the truck to take them elsewhere for their walk. When we returned, the bear was gone.

We both woke bolt-upright in the night. Our dogs were losing their minds again, barking and hurling themselves against the slider. There was a muffled crack from next door, followed by a blue flash soaring over our driveway.

"Flares. Probably trying to scare him off," said the husband. "Not the worst idea."

"I guess," I said. "Unless it sends him over here."

It was a moonful of an evening, and it was easy to pick out the silhouettes of houses, fences, and trucks. Another flare went off, the burst of bright outlining the bare branches. I paced around the house, took a few sock-footed steps onto the front porch, and sniffed. The across-the-street neighbor's living room held the vibrating glare of a television. The green plastic add-on room of the old lady's trailer glowed. It was as if our neighborhood could only reach its full vigor when we had no sun in our eyes.

"Want to watch some TV?" asked the husband.

"Something not scary," I said. "A *Seinfeld*?"

We dozed together on the couch as if we were people who still sought out each other's company.

I'd seen the divots in the dirt made by those claws.

"No dog makes a print like that," our garbage man had said, "even a big old part-wolf one." Long, scrappy pieces had been carved from the shed that held the trash bins, leaving piles of shreds and strips of fresh wood. "They know right where to go, the bears do," he said. "The area around the handle, scratching and whacking until the whole lock-thing wobbles off. Keeps Away Bears, my ass."

All this bear-talk made us feel hardcore; it was our regional duty to be cavalier. We boasted about our power outages and how we were one of the last spots in the lower forty-eight to get off dial-up, happily tolerating phone lines that screeched as if haunted. We were proud to stockpile canned beans, bags of rice, and ten-gallon jugs of water. When our old friends from the city used words like *hinterlands*, we flipped it into a compliment.

I woke, alone on the couch, to the chaos of police megaphones and flashers. The husband's boots were gone from the mat. He'd also taken his coat and the lantern we kept by the door for when the electric went. The sagebrush along the road was lit up orangey-red, and if the pulses hadn't been so rhythmic, it would have looked like our yard was on fire.

An officer stood in our drive next to a sedan with its doors open, the searchlight pointed into the scrub. Each of my neighbors' yards had their own police car and light show. I remember wondering if our town could have this many cops or if some of these guys were on loan.

Our dogs were trying to dig their way through the wooden front door. I pictured the scrapes, smaller versions of the ones the bears leave on fruit trees, garbage sheds, and cars when someone forgot to bring in the to-go leftovers. Another officer came from around the side of the house with my husband, who yelled at the dogs to shut-the-hell-up in a voice so high-pitched and shaky that I knew it was bad.

"Heart attack," said the officer who had twice pulled me over, both times giving me a warning and calling me "Hon." He had a rifle slung over his shoulder and a dart gun at his side.

"She wouldn't have stood a chance," said the other, who I recognized from the gym. "Weird though. They never go near people," he said. "Or rarely do." He pulled on his collar and looked for an instant towards the old lady's trailer. I hoped they wouldn't ask if I'd seen any signs of the bears coming in this close, and I wondered if I'd lie.

They didn't find the bear that night or any other. We got four inches right after, and there were no tracks in the snow, except for jackrabbits and coyotes. That bear had left us. We let the dogs run free and got casual about strapping our garbage bins. Every now and then,

I'd look at the pictures we took, clear and crisp. The bear's pink tongue, the azure sky. Our yard, our tree.

Those young men, whoever they were—the grandsons, I guessed—came with two pickups, the sides bolstered with planks and wire, to cart away the tiny woman's belongings. An enamel-top table, several carved santos, a single dresser. When they took away the curtains, I could see straight through the trailer to the mountain on the other side. Framed that way, it reminded me of motel paintings, flattened and uninspired.

The home would soon enough be stripped of its copper wire and plumbing, the door left unhooked to smack against the siding when the wind kicks up. The metal building would rust and crumble under the weight of the snow left piled on its roof with no heat from inside to melt it away. It would either be mythologized or ignored into the landscape along with the likes of disused herders' cabins and chicken coops that dot the terrain out this way.

When the realtor came to take pictures of our house, she stood strategically in the road so as not to show the buckling trailer.

"Everyone knows the story," she said. "I'll see what I can do. Maybe someone from away." *Like yourselves,* she did not say. The ads she placed called us "highly motivated sellers," and we knew we would take a hit. In my head, I divided that number by two.

A PILE OF STUFFED ANIMALS

The animals started being delivered as soon as Chad had moved in, if you could call it that. The moving in consisted of him being there more than not, followed by him being there all the time. Sometimes, Julia would tip the UPS guy because he had to get out his UPS-brown dolly to maneuver the deliveries up onto her already-sagging porch. He'd tilt it forward to encourage the massive boxes to slide off, and then, as the wooden landing creaked, the burden successfully shifted, he'd exhale. Other times, feeling she should have some explanation on hand, Julia hid.

The crates were ridiculously heavy. Built custom and can't be thrown out, so said Chad. They were stacked all over the place. The windows obstructed, the perimeters closing in, the house became a cave. She felt she was becoming a nocturnal creature, strange and elusive, while Chad bumped around, humming his songs and refusing to comment.

He unpacked the animals one day while Julia was at work. She came home exhausted, and there was a lopped-off deer head on the kitchen table, one glassy eye checking her out, the other pointed toward the ceiling. The head had been taxidermied or whatever, because it didn't stink, but it was still gross. There was a new gash on the tabletop, nasty and antler-shaped. Under the table were two little foxes and a rat-like something. Maybe a ferret. The animals were everywhere. The house, *her* home, was a nasty diorama of desperation. Hers, not his.

Chad was a solo act, of the country-western flavor. You are so lucky, Julia's girlfriends said, tapping their crimson nails on the jewel case of his newest CD. The picture on the cover was, Julia guessed, about a decade old, and who had a CD player anymore? Still, a warm body is a warm body. Among this veritable zoo of cold bodies, that is.

One morning Julia saw the UPS man at the coffee place. Poor guy, she thought, having to drag all those deliveries across her rock-infested yard, around the corner of the corral, then over to the front of the house. She wondered if someone at UPS pulled the giant bolts off of the crate lids, just to be sure. That all along he's known, but what can he do? He's the UPS guy, and he had a job to do. She did as well, if only she could get up her nerve.

"How are you today?" the UPS guy said, not acting like Julia was strange at all.

She knew that he knew. She didn't find him that attractive, but his treating her like an everyday person who didn't have a lunatic freeloader living at her house made her feel a little flustery.

"Fine," she said, or maybe didn't, trying to remember how people who don't have stuffed kangaroos in their laundry room talk to one another. She looked out the café window. Several dust-covered cars created a horizon, and across the lot the sun still sat fairly low. Even this early, everyone still on their first cup, the air wiggled above the tops of the cars. "Maybe it will rain," she said, trying to remember rain, the grey-purple of a full cloud, almost coming up with a recollection of the smell of wet mud.

"That would be good," he said. "Although some of these roads—the unpaved ones—are tricky with a loaded truck."

She pictured the brown truck fishtailing, skidding sideways, a wooden crate escaping out of the back door, a stuffed armadillo rolling out of the fractured mess, then coming to rest with its creepy, burnished toenails pointing towards the wide, wide sky.

The smaller animals Julia could carry. In the wheelbarrow, she put the medium-sized ones: a fox; some raggedy bird, black with chewed-up feathers; and a snake. She could have sworn they were multiplying as she tried to move them all. On her last trip through the house, Chad's snoring seeped from the bedroom.

They were all out in the yard now, except the emu that lay on the blue tile floor in the bathroom. She'd need help with that one, it was so oddly shaped. But she'd figure something out, even if she needed to saw the damn bird in half. The deer's antler had ripped a hole in the leg of her shorts, but she didn't even care. She wiped away a sweaty clump of fur, the dust on the back of her hand becoming a muddy smear. The sign Julia nailed to the fence post near the pile stated simply: FREE.

In time, the UPS man will happen by, crateless, perhaps tipping his index finger off the steering wheel as he passes the end of Julia's drive.

TIRE

The pop was barely audible over Julian's wailing. Francie expected the careening sideways, as well as the downward shift as the car slid off the paved road. The landing, pitched forward and tilted toward the passenger side, she did not.

She looked through the frame of the windshield into the last light. The browned field was a watercolor in shades dreamier than real life. If this were a romantic movie, snow would begin to fall, all glimmer-edged and hopeful. But this was not that sort of thing, and Francie was not at all ready to think about the flat tire, here in the almost dark, somewhere vaguely near the Colorado border. A place so remote it has its own dialect, so off-the-map that census takers would just give up, and sometimes even go missing.

Then Francie remembered the back seat.

She swung her head around, and there was Julian.

Just sitting there. The slide seemed to have vacuumed the screaming right out of him. His cheeks were blotchy, and tears were balanced on the edges of his eyelashes. He smacked the bumper on the front of his car seat. "Car ride," said Julian.

Indeed, thought Francie.

Her sister, Jane, had dropped off Julian that morning, had Julian's seat out of her car and into Francie's before she could even form a good argument. "Good practice for you if you ever settle down," said Jane as she expertly wove the seatbelt behind the car seat and gave it a good shake.

The car seat was quite used, and Francie wondered where Jane got it from, some crazy barter or maybe off the side of the road. Francie liked her nephew a lot. He was the only member of her family to have the potential to be at all interesting, but this was the third time in a week that Jane dumped him on her without even asking.

"Your getting fired was the best thing that ever happened to me!" said Jane as she handed off the screaming toddler to Francie. "If he won't go to sleep, sometimes he'll pass out in the car. Just take him for a little ride."

"Laid off, Jane. Not fired," said Francie, tired of explaining the tenuousness of their rural economy to a person who barely participated in it, and, she thought, lots of folks in these parts were losing jobs, not just her. At least she'd had one to begin with.

So, she'd taken Julian for his little drive. "Just stay there, honey," Francie said to the toddler, pushing against the late autumn wind to get the car door open. That was half an hour ago, and a solid twenty degrees warmer.

Now, she didn't even need to look for traffic. Nothing comes through this pass except tourists and horse trailers, and it was the wrong season for both. She reached back in and flipped on the hazards anyway, just in case. You never know. And if someone did come through, for sure they'd stop for a lady and a baby in a stuck car, even an absolute beater like hers.

Francie stepped outside the car, and the skin on her face shrink-wrapped immediately. She surveyed the remaining shreds of the tire resting in a rut of frozen mud. Julian pressed his face flat on the window, stared at her. Condensation and residual snot framed his mushed-up nose and cheeks.

Francie had thought Julian seemed hot and sort of clammy when his mother handed him off so quickly, disappearing to God-knows-where. When she tried to calm him down, get him to eat something, he had just screamed. And screamed. Jane hadn't picked up her phone, and Francie realized that she didn't have any idea who Julian's pediatrician was. "You're not sick, right? Just crabby," she said to Julian, who calmed for an instant and stared at her, wide-eyed. He gulped and began to wail again. This was all Jane's fault. She always ignored things until they couldn't be remedied, then shoved them off on someone else. Jane had referred to her pregnancy as her beer gut until about six months when she finally went to a doctor.

Now that Jane was "back in the dating scene"— Jane's words, not Francie's—Julian seemed to be logging in quite a lot of time at homes other than his own.

"You just don't know how it is, being a single mom and all," Jane had said.

"No, no I don't," Francie had answered, but Jane was already gone.

Not that Francie was feeling particularly reliable at that moment, and even less so now as she tried to recall what she knew about this road. She had felt sure she was on Route 141 but had been so absolutely fuming that she hadn't paid much attention. She couldn't quite remember what she'd already passed. There were no landmarks other than a few snaky turns and their bullet-pocked warning signs. She was below the tree line, but only just. Was it hunting season? Francie wasn't sure. Everything was dead, besides the pines, which, thankfully, grew close enough together to hold back some of the wind. The silence felt like a lead weight.

It didn't matter where she was, having stomped out of the house with so little. No purse, not even a decent coat. At least Jane had put a jacket on Julian. It would be dark in twenty minutes and the temperature was plummeting. A buck stood in the field staring at her, lovely but useless.

She dug her way through the trunk looking for the spare, tossing the contents behind her. The supplies were more about snowy ditches than flat tires: rope, an ice scraper with a broken handle, a small collapsible shovel, a bag of cat litter. Francie dumped this mountain-dweller's assortment on the side of the road and wondered if it would become midden, evidence of sorts. She had thought herself the competent one. Two bottles of water, puffed and frozen, rested on the thin rubber tire. She exhaled. The tire was here. She could picture that tire lying in the driveway, accidentally left out, what she had feared most, but it must have made its way back into the car. A miracle. Such a good sign! Things would be fine, just fine, and when Jane returned, Francie would stand up to her, put an end to the free daycare service.

The buck watched her drop the tire near the front of the car. It spun and landed in an icy rut with a crunch. Julian had fallen asleep. She didn't open the car door, wanting to preserve the heat. She would simply change the tire and they'd be back on the road before he woke up.

She returned to the trunk to look for the tire iron and smacked her hand, hard, on a hunk of chain. She found the flashlight, its batteries dead. Eventually, she unearthed a monkey wrench, not the best solution, but maybe the only tool she had. Two of the nuts were very loose. The third she was able to get going by stepping on the handle of the wrench, using a bit of leverage. The fourth wasn't budging. She jumped on the handle a bit, felt the threads collapse under pressure, ruining the traction.

Francie sat down on the solid little tire, just for a moment. The day had ended swiftly, heading into a moonless, brittle night. She shut both eyes to adjust her pupils so that she might see better in the near darkness.

Francie wondered why she had even become so inflamed, to up and run off like she did. She couldn't even recall what her anger had felt like. Jane was going to be Jane, and neither Francie nor anyone else would be able to do anything about it. Everything except for herself, Julian, and the darkness had faded away. Her night vision had kicked in, so she could see clear across the field, past the dead grass waiting for the full-on winter.

She'd think. Rest and think. And figure how to get this tire off or come up with some sort of solution. She knew—was of—this land, and that had to count for something.

The buck was still there, waiting, or else in mirage. It wasn't as cold as she expected, seemed to be warming, even. She knew there wasn't enough gas to run the car through the night and that she couldn't carry Julian very far. He was safe and warm and conked out, for the moment. Perhaps there would be a hunter's blind or a warming hut nearby. Maybe some flares or lanterns, maybe even some food. No reason to wake him up. She'd just do a little half-mile survey to assess the situation. As Francie walked up the road, the deer tilted his head—the only witness. She took off her fleece jacket and tied it around her waist. She turned away from the road, following a scrubby path into the woods. She'd make pancakes for Julian when they got home—some nice comfort food, regardless of the time of day or night. Pancakes with a happy face made out of syrup. Jane could have some, too. She'd be appreciated. They would look like a happy family.

They found Julian the next day, the car out of gas, but the hood still warm. Wet, hungry, and dehydrated, all he could tell the officers was, "Car ride."

LESSON PLAN

after Donald Barthelme's "The School"

Eliza tapped on the aquarium glass with her pen. She scowled at the still-alive salamander. Conjured bad thoughts about him. Considered withholding crickets. He didn't look any worse, or even sick at all—whatever *that* would look like. Nor did the bullfrog or the gerbils or the turtle. Not even that stupid goldfish. This was unheard of, these small animals and their ridiculous longevity, and frankly, the timing was not good. Some tiny thing needed to keel over and soon, or else Eliza would have to give the Big Talk without a familiar-but-not-human point of reference. She just wasn't up to it. Not this week. It was too hot for this nonsense. Too dry to even sweat, let alone teach about mortality. The air felt overstuffed, and dust was everywhere. *I'll move to the desert,* she'd said. *It will be an adventure.* She had come here for lightness, but this latest could not be further away from that.

In a perfect world, the deceased would be fur-ry and cute, four-legged and named after someone's grandmother. The chicken wouldn't do, not with those creepy claws, nor would the silkworm pupas. They weren't really even pets. She never should have let the class name them. But that salamander, Mr. Magoo. Now, *he* was a contender. The kids seemed to like him a lot, while Eliza did not. Not one bit. He had the stick-ing-out eyes of a criminal: dark and never blinking. She suspected that lizards could live as long as humans. Wasn't that one of the factoids that little boys threw at her, year after year? Or maybe that was for turtles.

Perhaps she could find an already-dead pet, a white mouse or some such, like on Craigslist or from a lab. There were lots of weird experiments going on over in Los Alamos; for sure, there had to be an irradiated mouse or two. She peered in at the guinea pigs nibbling on apple slices, all happy, as far as she could tell. In fact, several of the animals were actually looking healthier, as if her classroom were a spa in Sedona. Their vigor was like a curse.

"You are going to have to talk to the a.m. kindergar-teners about death," Ruth, the principal, told Eliza. "And soon." And with that, Ruth squished away in her weird round-bottomed sneakers, slurping on the green swamp in the sweaty Ball jar that she marched around with every morning. Ruth was some sort of a profes-sional drudge and the lead antagonist in this nightmare.

Eliza decided to show the kids *The Lion King* as a warm-up. She wondered if it might be too abstract for five-year-olds, but once they started bawling, she knew she'd done the right thing. "Look guys, it's for your own good," she had said when she plopped the kids down on their hypoallergenic nap cushions. "Believe me, it's better this way."

Of course, some parents complained, but they always did. They were so sure their little nippers were simultaneously naïve and possessing genius of an order never before known. Three parents had actually used the word *zeitgeist* when extrapolating on their spawn's exceptional understanding of the workings of the world in the Other Things We Should Know About Your Child section of the application packet. Actually, all the school wanted to know was whether they were truly potty-trained and if their little heads would puff up like blowfish if there were a peanut in the building.

Despite all the ancillary nonsense, the being-with-the-kids part of the job was excellent. Kindergarten is a small window where children are mature enough to speak in full and comprehensible sentences and yet still were enthusiastic about almost everything. It was almost "graduation" time, and while she still loved them to bits, summer break was also looking pretty fine.

"Miss Eliza! Miss Eliza!" They ran towards her from all points in the schoolyard and huddled around her legs. Without her even asking, they lined up, eager to go into the classroom.

"We need to have a talk," she said, as she counted their little heads. "Has anyone lost, umm, maybe their grandpa?"

"Lost?" said the overly verbal Clarissa. "How could I lose my grandpa? I'm not in charge of him." Ruth appeared at the little square window of the classroom door and made a slicing motion across her throat. Eliza wasn't sure if this meant that she was fired or was supposed to kill something—that couldn't be it— or maybe Ruth was choking. If only.

Eliza made a point of having a student or two by her side at all times for the rest of the day. If Ruth came barreling towards her, Eliza would whisper *little ears*, which would deflect Ruth. But she couldn't forever use five-year-olds as her shield.

"What about we make voodoo dolls of the critters and then do bad deeds upon them?" Eliza's boyfriend, Revelry, said. "We can make them out of dryer lint and put googley eyes on and then have them meet sorry endings. I'll document it."

This was the week Eliza had scheduled to break up with Revelry. She was fed up with his everything-must-be-a-performance approach to what she felt were legitimate problems. He was forever taking her car, unairconditioned heap that it was, into the scrub to make this or that video about ghosts or hoodoos, or whatever. She promised herself that if he didn't on his own, and without prompting, *finally* admit that Revelry was not his given name and just cut it out already, then he was out of here. "That's not a name!" she screamed, but silently, in the mirror. She was getting too old for his I'm-an-artist-so-I-just-can't-help-myself antics.

When Revelry was awarded a genius grant on Tuesday of break-up week, Eliza lost her momentum. This grant, in the amount of $10,000, would allow Revelry time to spend his days archiving a soundwork consisting of the purrs, scratches, and other bodily sounds that their cat, Sylvia, made. Well, technically, Eliza's cat. So, far be it from her to interrupt his artistic vision. She'd have to let Revelry stay in order to give him continued access to his subject, or medium, or whatever poor Sylvia now was. She and the cat were art-hostages in their own home.

"I'll give you a credit on the recording as a co-art-ist," Revelry said. "Then you can write off Sylvia's food and cat toys." Eliza wondered when he began to know or care anything about money, since it was *her* teenie apartment, *her* food, *her cat*, and she was pretty sure that Revelry wouldn't know a tax return if it walked up and introduced itself. While sometimes the only apparent difference between him and her students was height, she gave him credit for sticking it out in a career that seemed like a massive gamble. She herself had changed her major from art to early childhood education after but one overwhelming term.

The Glorious Day School seemed, and in many re-spects was, an ideal teaching situation. But with each new round of applications, the parents became in-creasingly militant in their laid-backedness as well as in their neurosis. She had previously been unaware of the rich-neohippy-Southwest trajectory, but she soon found out, and worse: those people had kids. They al-ternately wanted their child to slide down their own super-duper-colorful inner rainbow and, in addition, be fully prepared for Princeton by the time they were eight. *Our Equinox will be attending school dressed as he pre-fers, in either surgical scrubs or with pants on his head. He will only eat foods presented in clusters whose units are prime num-bers. And he has written a sonata about Pangaea.* Or some such nonsense. In truth, the students were precisely unremarkable, each and every year. And that's what made them perfect.

There was often such a disconnect between her little charges—so innocent and blank-slate-like—and the agenda she needed to fulfill. Yet, somehow, *usually*, the tasks were met, if chaotically. Most years, a teacher could count on one or most of the classroom pets to come to an untimely and utterly random demise, even before winter break. Then everyone gets to learn their lesson about death, and they can then move on to hot lava. But these animals were proving to be problematic in their extreme health. These pets were *hanging on*.

"We've never gone four months—not even three—without some animal or another turning into a rock overnight," Brett, the other Kinder teacher said. "I usually check all of the aquariums before the kids get in." He had a tie-dye shirt for every day of the week and wore those shoes that have toes, but Eliza liked him anyhow. "You know," he said, waving the recess flag over his head, "this might be a record. Six months and no corpses."

"Yeah, well now I've got Ruth all over my case," Eliza said. "Death is on the lesson plan. Now, according to the little note she left me, I need to hurry it up."

"Miss Eliza! Miss Eliza!" Several little boys came screeching towards her, one holding a bloody baby tooth in his palm.

"Trevor! Your first tooth!" Her fervor implied that no one had ever performed so worthy a deed as losing a tooth. "Congratulations!" She looked over the boy's head to Brett, "Apparently this all has to go down soon, so if something turns up D-E-A-D in your room, will you please throw it into mine?"

"You got it, sweetie," said Brett, a true ally. He always got her burrito order right—green, no queso—and was decidedly team lose-the-art-guy. They'd had a plan, one they hatched over two-for-five margaritas (the cheap tequila, but still), that they would dump their respective boyfriends and begin their BEST LIVES, but Eliza had chickened out. Now Brett was alone and paying the rent for two, yet he still said, "Love ya best of all, babe," to Eliza every afternoon as she headed home.

When Eliza walked into her apartment the afternoon of her most recent warning from Ruth, she was surprised (but not) to see a cluster of Revelry's art-school buddies, all of them eight years out but still skinny and ironic in their muttonchops and lack of socks. The living room (in truth, the only room) was a salad of wires and discarded shrink-wrap.

"Eliza. Honey! Not just microphones. We got ceiling-mounted cameras!" Revelry said, pointing upward, which pulled his Cookie Monster t-shirt way up past his bellybutton. "Awesome or what?" Eliza had always liked that little strip of hair on his stomach. At the same time, she wished he'd stop dressing like a toddler. "We can stream everything. All Sylvia, all the time. We'll be famous."

"Know what? You just do whatever it is you're doing," Eliza said. "I'm going to go sit in the bathtub and weep." The evening cool had set in, but Eliza felt no less exhausted. She imagined a world where no one spoke to her for a solid forty-eight hours.

Once the drilling and hammering was over and Revelry's little crew left, he knocked on the bathroom door. "You okay?"

"I just don't get what the crisis is. Dead-animal emergency, says Ruth. Still. She just won't let up. Crazy crone. Can I just quit?"

"What about a decoy?" Revelry said. "I was at the pet store, you know, getting a little sumpin-sumpin' for Sylvia. Some of those toys look very authentic. So I got these." He pulled from the paper bag five greyish-brown catnip mice, which did look like real mice, sort of. If you squinted.

"I guess if I wave one at the kids from a distance," Eliza said. "Let Sylvia maul them up a bit."

He threw two of the catnip mice out the open door to the living room and Sylvia performed a flying pounce-tackle-roll combo. "How excellent. I hope the camera got that," Revelry said. "Hey, want some company?" Rhetorical, as his pants had already hit the floor. Revelry had a particular fondness for bathtub sex, which was fine with Eliza, except oftentimes she wondered if she had fractured a kneecap on the enamel tub. After, they could still hear Sylvia thumping around in the living room with the mice.

The next day Eliza had a paper bag with two roughed-up cat toys ready to go. But it was Fire Drill Day, and then it was time to go home. The day after was Music Day, stressful enough without the mice, with everyone wanting a turn on the drums. Then it was Friday, which meant a half-day, and she didn't want to enact her plan and then have the weekend wash it out of their jellylike minds.

"Nothing dead in my room," Brett said, on the way out, "or I absolutely would have tossed it onto your desk."

"Thanks for looking out for me," Eliza said. "You know, I can't but wonder if something else is going on. Why the urgency?" Ruth had stopped talking to Eliza.

"I'm thinking just wait. Something will drop soon."

So, things went on: the bags of mauled but unoffered toys, staring down the kindergarten pets, the drunken bathtub sex. And the hostile Post-its from Ruth, always unsigned. *The death talk is long overdue. Are you avoiding me??? We are on a schedule, and you need to keep to it. Are you replacing dead animals and lying to me?* Such a freak show, that Ruth was. Maybe Eliza should just lower Sylvia into the gerbil tank—instant Pamplona!

Meanwhile, Revelry was getting a bit of traction on the videos, which one of his friends was streaming for him, the upgrade from simply audio seeming to pay off. The guy would come by the apartment every now and then to adjust the sound or move a camera. Revelry's actual work input seemed minimal. Sure, he was on the computer a lot, but what did he actually do toward this "project" besides living in the same place as the cat and ordering takeout? Meanwhile, Sylvia took to her stardom as if she were born for it.

When a critic came to interview Revelry, he seemed more interested in Eliza than in The Sylvia Project. He didn't even want to meet the cat. "I don't much like animals," the reviewer said in a faux-British accent.

"Why did he keep calling me Sylvia?" Eliza asked after he'd left.

"I don't know. It was like I wasn't even here, the way he kept staring at you," Revelry said.

"Well, I for one thought he was a creeper."

Revelry opened the fridge and pulled out a bottle of wine. "Tub?"

"Sure, why not," Eliza said, rubbing the sides of her kneecaps. Revelry tossed a catnip toy into the middle of the room, and Sylvia launched herself from the couch.

So, this is my weird little life, thought Eliza. At least now they could afford classier wine.

In the morning, as usual, Revelry slept while Eliza raced around trying to piece together a teacherly outfit from the piles of clothes she'd left mouldering on the floor. Her phone rang every couple of minutes, but she ignored it for as long as she could stand it. When Brett called for the seventh time, she answered. "I sure hope you're calling about something dead."

"You may want to check out *The Weekly's* art section," Brett said. "Or not."

"Is Revelry reviewed?"

"Sort of. And remember, I'm only the messenger," Brett said. "You could always move to the mesa, go off grid."

"Stop it," Eliza said. "Give."

"Apparently the cat movie is getting internet play. One could say a bit much, if one was a private sort of a person. Who has a job where they are in charge of, say, impressionable youths," he said. "And frankly, I would not have pegged you for a howler."

"Howler?" Eliza knew nothing good could come of whatever he was going on about.

"Call me if you need a drink," Brett said, "I've got the uptown tequila here with your name on it." Eliza wondered what in the absolute hell he could be talking about. She scrolled backward through the last few days and couldn't come up with anything. She scratched and scratched her itchy neck.

The wind was really kicking as Eliza drove the highway to school. As she exited, a hunk of loose sagebrush scraped across the hood of her car. She was unable to name the dread moving through her. It felt like both panic and destiny.

When she got to work, Eliza tiptoed into her classroom, checking the animals for casualties, fully knowing she was the disaster. She felt pretty sure that Ruth didn't have the wherewithal to go online and watch Revelry's film with the horrid, *horrid* soundtrack of Revelry and herself in the background. In the bathtub. She really was a screamer. Who'd have guessed?

Not even Eliza herself. Of course, she'd agreed to have her name put on the project along with Revelry's. And, of course, that evil interviewer had linked his story to the site. And, of course, she'd mentioned her job, specifically naming The Glorious Day School in the interview. Maybe people wouldn't recognize the sounds for what they were. Maybe she'd levitate and land on another planet.

It was when the first parent came to drop off their spawn and wouldn't leave that Eliza knew it was all over: her job, maybe her teaching license, definitely her sense of decorum. Irate parents in suits and pricey athleisure outfits and scrubs and what looked like fancy witches' costumes all stood with their feet hips-width apart, their arms gripping their children's shoulders, unified. Eliza wondered which of them had first found the video. And then for how long did they keep it to themselves as a private nugget of entertainment? She had done nothing that each and every one of them hadn't done, except for having a clueless boyfriend with numbskulls for friends.

She could hear Ruth squishing towards her. The doom about her was palpable and, sadly, was not about the critters.

As Eliza wrote out her letter of resignation, Ruth stood over her to make sure she did it right. Every thirty seconds or so, Eliza's phone vibrated and danced along her desktop. Another frantic text from Revelry. And the promises: No more art! No more technology! He'd replace their claw-footed tub with a tiny shower that very day! He meant well, her art-boy. But the way he just bumped along, happily and with no consequences, it was infuriating. Maybe she couldn't live in tandem with that level of carefreeness. Meanwhile, the pets ran around in their habitats, all cute, chewing and pooping, the way they'd always done.

LIKE SALMON ON THEIR WAY HOME

Fred, Luanne's little brother, had asked for the coffee at the airport, assuring her that he drank it all the time. She knew that had to be untrue. She wasn't sure of her role with Fred, given the fraying state of her family. Rescuer, parent, friend, sibling? Kidnapper, maybe? She had zero experience in any of these. She'd flown out of the tiny Albuquerque Airport, which had been branded The Sunport, all through college and grad school, but this time was different. Though she wasn't sure anymore which direction was the return—this particular flight had a finality to it, as if things could no longer be the same.

There had been a three-hour delay for wind shears—why didn't they call it The Windport?—which was hardly news. And now, finally queued up and boarded, she was spiriting Fred off to California. Not that many, or any, ten-year-olds take in coffee as part of their morning ritual, but she hadn't wanted a battle. They had both just lost their father, and in some ways, their mother, so she had relented, now regretting it when he started thrumming the hand rest.

She knew he was dying to go to the restroom but would never admit it. He was too formal, too awkward to talk about anything related to the body. She touched his shin, which made him jerk. She was only trying to signal he needed to stop pressing his feet against the seat in front of him. The guy slumped there had turned around and scowled twice, and she saw from his reflection in the window that he was still pissed. If getting kicked by her little brother was this guy's biggest problem, then he was lucky.

"Once we're at such-and-such altitude, you can go to the back," she said. "A bell will ring and the seatbelt sign will go off."

"I know," Fred said. "I've been on a plane before." Even this was something she hadn't known. He'd been appalled when she said she'd hold onto his boarding pass. "In case of what?" he said and ripped it out of her hand, slicing a neat little papercut through the meat of her index finger. "Thank you for your service," he said to the attendant who took the ticket. He marched down the tunnel to the plane as if he were a businessman with a million frequent flyer miles.

She had little knowledge of children, less so of her brother. He was something like a curious gnome to her. A few years ago, he'd gone through a stage when he would only wear beige. "Too colory," he'd said as she tried to talk him into a blue sweater when she'd taken him for a day of wandering around in Santa Fe during Christmas break. She thought a shopping trip would be something they could do together, but he got overloaded even before she did. He did not want a smoothie, did not want to eat at a chain that had an immense menu where certainly he could find something he'd like, and would not agree to wear the "very bright" blue sweater that was, in truth, close to light grey.

She'd been asked to take Fred out of the house because he was "tiring your father out," their mother said. Luanne noticed that her mother had made up one eye but left the other bare. At that moment, it seemed comical, but with time, Luanne realized it was a sign of something—of what, she just couldn't figure. Her mother seemed to be on her own orbit, veering away from them all, unable or unwilling to complete everyday tasks. Maybe she was just distracted, Luanne told herself. However, deep down, she knew it was something more, that her mother had been forced to be the connective tissue between these people, her family, none of whom really knew each other. And her father, her stoic and competent father who never let an ounce of his true self show, was already fading. He had become soft around the edges, passive even.

Luanne always sensed Fred was an average kid—despite being picky and having a hard time making friends—but now she wondered if there was something more going on. She gathered that he wasn't unhappy so much as he seemed to be waiting for time to pass, that he perhaps knew something better was ahead. She felt disassociated from Albuquerque each time she left. She wondered if their hometown would feel strange to Fred once he was away from it. It was, after all, possible to both miss a place and feel alienated from it. She also wondered if anyone, a teacher perhaps, had sought to find out if there was something beyond his being odd.

She herself had left for college in a huff. Either way, travel back from California had been infrequent, and by grad school, home felt like a place she visited rather than somewhere she'd lived. Her brother had evolved into his ways without her. She had no idea what his habits were, but they were sure to be odd. They looked enough like each other that people assumed they were related but weren't sure how. Their ages fell somewhere between siblings and parent-child. Both of them had been surprises, Luanne when her folks were way too young and Fred when their parents had long assumed she would be an only child. Sometimes she told people they were cousins, just to shut it down. On earlier visits, she let people who couldn't do simple math believe he was her child, and on occasion, his curious behavior garnered them favors. Immediate seating at a crowded restaurant, free popcorn, and on this day, they were asked if they needed to pre-board, hinting at some limitation on Fred's part. This probably was due to his carry-on, a battered briefcase, and his aviator glasses, which looked like they came from the old-man rack at the optician's. She worried that Fred might be mature enough to pick up on people's sense that he was different, and this made her want to champion him. In fact, she knew they did, because adults said things right in front of him as if he were intellectually impaired or deaf. Kids just stayed away.

"What do you picture California will be like?" she asked, but the bell went, and Fred leapt over her. Was she supposed to walk him back to the bathroom? No one could grab him—they were midair after all. When he was back there for so long, she hoped he didn't bother the crew or lock himself in the john.

Luanne had done this flight plenty of times, back and forth for undergrad, and now law school, and enjoyed passing over the changing landscape. Desert, then mountains, more mountains, then the Pacific. She had spent a certain amount of her first year of law school willing herself into a trance, biding until she escaped or didn't. She spent a lot of time prone on the floor, her favorite spot being the library basement. With her cheek against the cold cement, she'd sighed, dreaming of an exit plan that didn't involve too much shame. She likely was depressed, a thing that was not an option, according to her father. "Depression is just a New Agey word for sleeps too much," he'd said when she tried to confide in him.

She'd lay there, between the forgotten stacks, still as a dead fish, her exhales pushing fluffs of dust toward the lesser-used volumes. Louisiana Common Law, Wyoming cattle-grazing statutes, a few outdated briefs on riparian rights. Everything useful was now available electronically. The library was just a three-story study hall. A repository for anxiety.

Neither the top nor the bottom of her class, she had not formed any alliances. The basement was a respite from her aggressive classmates, edging and gossiping, always loud and so sure of themselves. They instinctively formed study groups and played intramural softball, which was an excuse to whack each other on the shins. The one low-key guy, the son of a big-deal judge, had not returned after Thanksgiving break. Supposedly, he had joined the Peace Corps, a thing Luanne had been surprised to hear still existed. He was someone she'd thought could have been a friend, a fellow malcontent. She couldn't imagine what her own father would have done if she'd headed off to Cameroon or Fiji. She couldn't imagine herself brave enough to pull such a move.

She acquired a bad boyfriend, because why not, and he broke up with her with enough regularity to keep things interesting—one time simply because a blonde stewardess had agreed to go out with him. "I never thought this could happen, a blonde, a real blonde," he'd said, as if she was to share in his good fortune. "She's not that smart though," he'd said. "Also, she's super young." Luanne shed not a single tear on that one. She was more disappointed that he'd chosen such a cliché than she was over the actual fact of being dumped.

She'd taken up running—for the rush but also to pass the time—the only good thing she'd gotten from the bad boyfriend. She loved the way she was turning to sinew. She turned out to be quite good at it, her temperament perfect for half-marathons. She joined a running club and told everyone she was a stewardess, a thing not one person believed. Whenever she stretched out after her run, she thought of him, the bad boy-friend. She stopped with the stretches and got plantar fasciitis.

When the blonde punctured a lung on a ski trip, the bad boyfriend called and expected, what—sympathy? "It could have been you," he said, which was confusing because she didn't ski, and they'd never gone anywhere together. In the middle of the night, he turned up thinking he'd get some sort of a pity fuck on the scratchy, rust-colored carpet of her apartment. Sure, that floor had seen several doses of torrid make-up action, but with the stewardess still in the hospital, it felt gross. Plus, this wasn't going towards any kind of a reunion. She realized, finally, she was a placeholder. Through the closed door, he either said, "It took me a long time to get over you," or "It *will* take me a long time to get over you," two very different things.

Around this time, she started getting phone calls from Fred. He'd call her after school, and she always made herself free to pick up.

"Have you seen *E.T.*?" Fred asked.

"Sure. I guess," she said. "A long time ago. Is that the one with the bike and the M&Ms?"

"Watch it for me, will you?"

"Sure, sure," Luanne said. "What's going on at home?"

"Oh, I don't know, no one's ever here," he said. "I think I'm either the boy, Elliot, or the E.T." Luanne watched the movie, and couldn't decide which character Fred was, or why he thought the movie bore any relationship to him.

Luanne wondered if he was a latchkey kid these days, or if that was even a thing anymore. He sounded alone there in the house, melancholy and bored, eating sandwiches and watching old movies. She tried to remember to call him more and found they had little to talk about. There was always *E.T.* "I don't know. Maybe you should come home," Fred said. "If you can."

Luanne glanced at her brother, who'd fallen asleep on the tray table somewhere over the Inland Empire. "Hey, Fred," she said, shaking him. "We're landing." He had a twee puddle of drool coming across his cheek, and his hair had gotten crazy in just the few hours. If he were someone else's problem, Luanne might have found him adorable.

"Let's see things right away," he said, as if their time was limited. In truth, no one was coming for him. Her family had been reshaping itself all along, each of them their own barely functioning unit. Perhaps, Luanne thought, she and Fred could form some reinvented version of family. Even now, she felt so alone that she could barely picture their parents' faces.

"I never got to ride on an airplane with Dad, you know," he said. "Let's pretend we're on a family trip," Fred said. "I mean, that would have been fun, wouldn't it?" He turned towards the window. If he was crying, Luanne couldn't tell.

This is it. We're it, thought Luanne. And she knew that Fred knew—probably better than she did.

The traffic out of Oakland Airport was clogged, as usual. "Are you sure you're not too tired?" Luanne asked. He'd slept, but still, they'd gotten up so early to get to the airport for their many-times-delayed flight.

Fred said he wanted to go out to eat. "Something I've never had before, " he said.

Who was this kid? Not the brother Luanne had ever seen. "You don't have to do that," she said, remembering how at their father's Christmas work party, the last time they were all together in a celebratory manner, Fred would only eat the shrimp cocktail. He refused all other offerings from the potluck, mostly tamales and enchiladas—the usual stuff in aluminum trays, made by somebody's abuela, and the many sets of chips and salsa that the lazy people brought. In the end, Luanne took repeated, sneaky trips to the long, decorated table to get enough mini goblets to make up a meal for him. When Santa showed up in a lowrider, Fred refused to have his picture taken along with all the other employees' kids. Later, when an unwitting coworker of their father's dragged Fred into a conga line, he became so upset that he fled to the bathroom and spent the rest of the evening sitting on the floor of one of the stalls.

Now, the traffic easing a bit, Fred was jumpy, looking around in all directions. Luanne figured he'd never seen this many cars at once, never imagined buildings this close together. She worried he'd feel claustrophobic, the way she had when she first moved here. He fired question after question at her, which she hoped was interest rather than panic. Had she been to the Port of Oakland? Were there ships? Would there be palm trees? Had she ever felt an earthquake? "I want to start living my life," he said, a line Luanne was sure he'd picked up from one of the movies he'd watched. She wondered if he examined the scene over and over, trying to dissect its meaning, the way he had to figure out if he was Elliot or E.T.

"Same," she said, wondering what her own life would be, now with all this. "Let's do Indian, then." She was only testing him, but he smiled back.

"Yesssss," he said, pumping his fist in a way that, again, wasn't in line with anything she knew about him.

"So, should you call Mom?" Luanne wondered if their mother was at all worried about Fred. "Or should I?" She was so drained by her father's death that she was oblivious to her mother's increasingly hollowed-out demeanor.

Even as far back as the Christmas party, their mother had seemed more distracted than usual. She didn't notice Luanne was hoarding the shrimp cocktails and would not join in the grousing about the tidbits thrown to the staff under the guise of holiday bonuses.

In retrospect, Luanne saw her mother was there only bodily, and it had been this way for some time.

"Nah," said Fred. "Mom doesn't notice me anymore, especially since Dad got sick. I think she was relieved that you took me."

"I'm sure that's not true," Luanne said, without confidence. "I think she's just exhausted." Luanne suspected their mother's ambivalence went much deeper. She didn't want to say depression, it sounded so medical, but still, she could not help but think of it. She'd seen it in others; law school attracted a subset of people who fed on misery. She had not yet admitted it about herself. Her wrong reasons for being there were different, but not uncommon. Something as stupid as making her father notice her, which she had decided was futile. At the party, a steady stream of coworkers came by her family's table, told her how proud he was of her and that he would sometimes tear up when asked about her, amazed that he could have sired such a genius. Meanwhile, he had never once told her such a thing.

And now, well, all kinds of regrets were surfacing, and Luanne hated that it took her father's death for her to begin to understand them.

Maybe their mother *didn't* notice Fred gone. She'd unraveled fully when their father was taken to the hospital and didn't ever regain herself. She stopped talking to Luanne and Fred, only conversing with the doctors, but never seeming to absorb what they were saying. Luanne felt she and Fred were silent witnesses—just there to take up space. Their mother focused on unimportant factors, like the parking garage rates and whether Luanne had locked the door at the house, instead of the doctor's assurances that they had done all they could. That their father's collapsing at the party was a symptom, not the disease, and that "inoperable" meant just what it sounded like. Their mother had weird, inappropriate bursts of optimism, giddiness even, and was given tranquilizers, probably too generous a dose, which left her even less in touch with the situation. Luanne was still mad at her mother for not telling her that her father was as ill as he was.

After the funeral, when it was suggested that her mother needed some time to "regroup," there was no argument to be made. Luanne hadn't checked in on them much until the spring term was over except for the few phone calls about movies with Fred, and by the time she made it back to visit, he was essentially on his own.

When she was packing to go back, Fred sat on her bed and looked at the floor, out the window, everywhere but at her. "Can't you stay?" he asked.

"No. I have to get back," she said, which was an absolute lie. Fred didn't answer, just hummed a little, then left her room. Like he had expected her answer. Her leaving him. She knew she had to do something but wasn't sure what.

"What if you came with me," Luanne said to Fred. She grabbed him in the hall, guided him into his room, and sat on his bed. His room was E.T. everything. She'd gotten him a bedspread and pillows off eBay, but there were other things. Figurines, a beach towel, pajamas crumpled on the floor. Things that she thought were too old to be easily acquired.

Luanne considered that she was on break, and could probably, maybe, ditch her clerking job. This was an unexpected relief—the hope of a small freedom from doing what she was expected to do on her pre-programmed law school trajectory. An excuse to not sit in an over-air-conditioned office all day counting the minutes until she could leave and go take a run. She figured she had just enough in her account to swing an unemployed summer, but only just. Or maybe she didn't, but the idea of this quick, unplanned decision was exhilarating, a figurative cliff-dive, even if she was—just maybe—using her father's death, her mother's whatever-was-going-on, and her brother's alone-ness as an excuse.

"To California?" He looked both terrified and elated. He looked around the room, as if to wonder if he could leave all this. "I don't wear them anymore," he said nodding at the pajamas. "They're kid stuff." He petted the bedspread, then sat down. Perched there, he reminded Luanne of a posed picture of herself, before he was born, taken at a strip mall. As he did now, she'd looked to be trying to convince herself of happiness, as if a person could smile an authentic smile on command.

"It doesn't matter. So, what do you think?" She had no idea how he was seeing their mother, if he was paying attention or if he was old enough to interpret what was happening. The brutal fact of their father gone and their mother's fraying. That he was de facto parentless.

"Yes." he said. "Like a vacation?"

"Sure. A vacation." Let's just call it that, she thought. Luanne wondered if he had any sense of what was going on, that their family was in shards. Could he have already developed their familial trait of acting like things were fine, ignoring and ignoring some more, even after they had escalated to a crisis? Now, after these ridiculous words had flown out of her mouth, and Fred had agreed to them, she realized she'd made some sort of a social contract with a ten-year-old. An odd ten-year-old whom she barely knew. She'd have to follow through. She had no idea what this meant on the day-to-day. What was his bedtime, did he eat like a regular person now, could she leave him alone for an hour while she took a run?

She couldn't backtrack, even once she realized the idiocy of this whimsical idea that she'd sweep him off for an adventure. She had to deal with a few technicalities, and quickly. Luanne knew she'd need proof to get him onto an airplane. This part she knew how to arrange. Their mother signed the temporary guardianship papers a little too quickly. "Oh, you know, in case I need to take him to the doctor, or something," she'd said, as their mother signed a sloppy scrawl and exhaled a sigh that sounded like relief. She was under some medication or another, Luanne didn't know what, and she knew any decent attorney could contest this transfer of rights, well, rights *and duties*. She also knew that no one would challenge her, least of all their mother. How easy this was, Luanne thought. How so like slippage. Even though her mother was in such a bad way, Luanne wanted her to put up some sort of fight. Luanne felt like some kind of fraudulent superhero, coming in to save the day via trickery.

Fred slept the rest of the ride from the airport, missing the inevitable gridlock. Luane shook him awake, "This is it," she said. "If you're still up for Indian." She opened the door to the restaurant, setting off a bundle of tinkly bells.

"It's very bright," Fred said as they waited for a table.

"But I like it," he added, checking himself. It used to be a single food cart, then three, roaming around the city at lunchtime, the locations trackable online. Now it was a tin building that felt very much like a blown-up food cart and an attached grocery, but upscale. The curry smells folded around them. "Is this like India?" he asked.

"No, I doubt it," Luanne said, ticking the least spicy dishes, adding a lassi and extra cucumber and yogurt side, and handing the card in at the counter. When they ate, she could see he was doing his best to act like this was his every day, and she pretended she didn't notice when he spat a chomped-up wad of chickpeas into his napkin. He was trying, in his own way, to march into his new life. Whatever she was doing at ten, it certainly was not this.

At her apartment, he didn't see the piles of laundry, the sad view into the back parking lot, the ragged couch he'd be sleeping on. "Maybe let's pretend we're adults and we're roommates," he said. "We have jobs and lots of friends and we're so busy we sometimes don't have time to go home. Also, we're on vacation and we're going to drive somewhere new to surf." Luanne had no idea where all this was coming from. She tried to think of a movie with lots of friends, and the surfing. This kid who, back home, refused to hike was now going to go in the ocean?

"Okay, sure," she said, thinking that kind of life could be nice. She wasn't going to argue. He was exhausted. They both were. The flight, the last few days, the wanton decision-making, had taken a lot from the both of them.

"Maybe you could put *E.T.* on your computer so I

could listen while I go to sleep?"

This she could do. After tricking their mother into relinquishing him and having dragged him across multiple state lines without a plan, she, of course, could provide him the movie. He was asleep before she could even queue it up. His face slack, he looked gentle and without a care.

He yelled in his sleep just the once. Luane's heart jumped—it felt ready to fly out of her throat. The impulse to take Fred was the right one, it had to be. She emailed their mother that they had arrived, but she had no expectation of a reply. She'd gotten a flood of messages from the bad boyfriend, which she erased like they were spam. If Fred could try new food, she could do that, at least. The last one made her heart jump. "ARE YOU OK" screamed the header. How dare he. She jammed her finger on the delete button.

Fred woke up quite early, and Luanne realized his body clock was still set for school one time zone to the east. "Let's go to a coffee shop," said Fred, ready for his new life. "You know, hang out, and then go to the beach." Like they were in a sit-com.

"What's with all the beach business?" Luanne asked, wondering if *E.T.* had beach scenes, pretty sure it didn't. "The beaches here aren't the way you think they are. They aren't warm, and the water's rough."

"I just want to see it, okay? See it and go in."

"Sure, sure. Let's do the coffee and some food, and I don't know, maybe see what kind of clothes you brought. Maybe get settled in more, like get groceries." Or maybe the opposite. Maybe take that vacation within the non-vacation they were in. Hit the coast road, pretend they had no cares. Get Fred a little wetsuit and a boogie board. Look for that fresh surf. Who knows—maybe they'd see dolphins.

What would it be like to cruise Highway One with her brother riding shotgun? She knew none of this anymore, could not even guess. She wanted to grab him and run, not as some sort of a savior, but as an act of apology. She wanted, desperately, to know what to say once Fred was ready to talk about their father's passing away, their mother's issues. She wanted him to be mad at her for ever going away.

Whenever people took this trip, they always headed south, towards the warmth. She could picture it, the Pacific on their right, mile markers in the margin. For this reason, they'd drive north.

PLAIN PERSON

I was tailing a truck piled high with furniture and parts of things that were about 2 percent away from being crap. The pickup's sides were bolstered by planks and chicken wire. It had no brake lights or side mirrors, and when he hit a T-junction, the driver used his arm to signal the turn, after which I was still stuck behind him. It was too wide for me to pass, but as I suffer janky-truck-specific road rage, I did anyway, spraying gravel from the corduroyed edge. An old man was driving, and a younger guy, maybe his son, was in the passenger seat. A woman sat between them, staring straight ahead. Her jaw locked, she was scared or mad, or so I believed. I felt my shoulder strap was strangling me as I imagined her body was my body, wedged between those men on this single-lane road going north.

Some ten minutes later, I hit the only gas station

on that entire stretch and pulled into the lot, knowing there wouldn't be another for hours. The New Mexico-Colorado border—you can get miles and miles of nothing if you don't watch out. The store smelled like bleach and was barely stocked. It seemed like they had changed owners: new pegboard and hand-printed signs.

The truck pulled into the station while I waited for the restroom. The older man delivered the woman to the line. She was dressed the Plain People way: brown ankle-length skirt, man's shirt, hair pulled back tight under a bonnet.

"I'll meet you right here when you get out," the old man said with his lips next to her ear.

She flinched and stared down at her huge boots with no socks, the laces pieced together from different bits. When he let go of her wrist, there were red marks left by his fingertips.

She could have been fifteen or thirty. I tried to make eye contact, like we were two women who understood each other's lives. When I did this, her neck mottled red. I suspected she was not accustomed to being seen, yet who was I but someone who'd run to the wilderness to hide from my own life. There are so many kinds of aloneness. And even more varieties of danger.

I wanted to ask if she was okay—even though I knew nothing about her, whether she'd been forced to marry the old man and work his ranch as free labor. I was just making things up. I'd heard accusations about these folks: the child brides, the isolation, the many children, but you never know what to believe. You make presumptions about who's in need of salvation.

I thought about saying, *Come with me, I'll rescue you,*

as if I could be some sort of a hero. As if I had a better idea of how to be a woman in the world. My crisis response was getting a radical haircut and moving across the country. I could recognize a woman who carried herself as if she had already surrendered to her fate.

Instead, I mumbled something about snow or the road or whatever you say to people so that you can feel like a human. I stamped my feet on the concrete slab floor, hoping to warm them, and noticed her boots were no less sturdy than my own. She said nothing, but the edges of her mouth tipped upward, or maybe just shifted.

When I came out of the bathroom, I held the door for her. Our eyes met, for a microsecond. The younger man had come to stand by her. There was a kind of ease between them. I got an awful coffee in a Styrofoam cup, fussing with the creamer packets. It is no accident that I did not see which way the truck went.

This Snow, This Day

The doctor wore a tweed blazer, his outfit for giving out bad news, which he scheduled for Fridays. Good news, would there have been any, was delivered by a phone call from his secretary, a thing that might happen any day of the week. She's a mumbler, but you can still get the gist from her tone—or from the fact that it's her on the line. Those times that the doctor didn't wear the suit jacket, he wore scrubs, changing them at lunch, whether they were soiled or not. Occasionally, he'd forget that he was still wearing them at the end of his long day, and then he could be seen in the wild in his green drawstring pants and matching V-neck that showed too much chest hair. He moved about town as if not covered in blood.

There was a tunnel from his office to the hospital, which people in town referred to as The Habitrail. Every now and then, he'd run through the hall from surgery and put the blazer on over the scrubs. This was his emergency news-delivering outfit, which he thought, incorrectly, was a reassuring look. I can promise you, it was not.

My appointment was on a Monday. Because I had been on vacation, I missed the usual Friday. The delivery of my news threw us both off schedule.

I wore ski pants, just in case. Not one for meditation, at least the sitting-still kind, I prefer to hit the slopes—just eight miles from my home—when I have something to think or not think about. I remember feeling obtrusive when the swishing broke the waiting room stillness as I walked down the hall to his office. The pants were magenta, a color I am not at all drawn to.

"Cancer," he said only once, and would manage to never say the word again, thereafter using the word *malignancy* and, eventually, simply: *it*. In his jacket with all that chest hair showing, my doctor informed me that intestinal surgery was in order. He slid a square box of tissues across his desk towards me. "It is a big surgery," he said, twice. I wondered where the line lay between big and little surgery. I felt like a robot for not crying, but I was not raised to be dramatic. My people are stoics and cynics, the kind of people who would deny such a thing as a *little* abdominal surgery.

"I'll show you if you want," he said, pointing to his shelf of thick books. They appeared to have been well read, which could only be good. Unless, of course, they'd come from a garage sale and were published in the 1930s.

"Yes, please," I said, not because I didn't have a basic understanding of how my insides were arranged, but because I wanted very much to see what a hunk of intestine separate from its person looked like. I pictured penne pasta or rigatoni, but pinkish-red. Whoever had his office before him must have been substantially taller because my doctor had to stretch so much for that huge book that I almost stood up to get it for him—and I'm not tall at all.

"Do you get queasy?" he asked. I told him that I once bagged a digit when my brother lopped off part of his finger in the spokes of a dirt bike, so not to worry. You put the piece in a bag and then that bag inside of another one filled with icy water. I was fifteen, and to this day I have no idea how I knew to do this.

He opened the book—very large and official looking—and pointed to a black and white illustration that was almost lovely, like an etching. I looked at his fingernails: short, but not chewed, and very clean. My own had been nibbled—gnawed upon, as if by a miniature beaver—a behavior I had developed within the last week.

I had thought it would be a picture, a photograph of the real thing. "That's a drawing," I said. "A cartoon." This was a great disappointment.

"You don't really want to see what it looks like," he said. I felt a wall go up, a thin one, but still. Doctor on one side, crackpot on the other.

I did want to see it, very much so. I felt that if the procedure and my insides could be made more real to me, if I could see those parts to which I had no access, then I would have some sort of agency. No, not agency, but understanding. I've always been a visual person. Language has never come first to me, so my way of grasping the elusive has always consisted of a ricocheting translation between the two modes.

He then said a bunch of not-too-helpful medical

words, followed by talk of a hose being sliced in two spots and then the openings stapled together. What I took away was that he'd be cutting a section out of my intestines and rejoining the two ends. It felt logical.

On his big calendar festooned with Georgia O'Keefe-ish watercolors of the Southwest, we scheduled the surgery for the only day available for several months: Christmas Eve. "I do not want anything sitting there in me for that long," I told him, pleased that he wasn't letting a holiday get in the way of the thing in my belly.

He unskillfully acted out the calming measures that he had been taught in medical school, despite my absence of hysteria. He talked about my relative youth, as compared to other patients similarly afflicted, and my excellent physical condition. *Except for that rotten part,* he didn't add. "You shouldn't need more than three or four months to be back to normal," he said, looking down at his hands. "Five, tops."

I'd been thinking two weeks.

"How much intestine will you remove?" I asked, counting in my head until February, then April, and picturing that hose.

"You'll still have plenty," was his weird response.

After I failed to weep or pass out, he walked me to the reception area. I put out my hand to shake his—I was raised to be polite to everyone, *no matter what*—and he gave me a blank stare and tipped his head to the side. It took him about five beats to return the gesture.

"I should learn to ski," he said. "Since I live here."

Yes. Yes, you should, I thought.

I made lists. I tried to picture the surgery. I fell into inexplicable giddiness. I considered my family's medical past but replaced that with thoughts of monochromatic places lit only by the Northern Lights. I decided it would be an excellent idea to run the half-marathon in Greenland the following June, imagining this goal to be realistic. I would wear clamp-on ice grips on my impulse-purchased, puffy, orange boot-sneakers. I could feel the bite and hear the ping and a little squeak as the prongs cut a divot in the ice, my foot twisting a bit with each stride. I considered what it would be like to be on a glacier and wondered if I'd be able to sleep where the sun doesn't set.

I tried to figure out how many ski days I had left until the big surgery. I made a mental calendar into the new year, guessing for how many alpine races I would need to find a substitute referee, wondering if I would be able to get in enough hours to keep my license, and calculated how many of my daughter's events I wouldn't see. My vision of the near future was reduced to mathematics, an effort to make it more palatable. I did not at that time wish to consider how one tells such a thing to an eleven-year-old, that there was this disease, that there would be surgery, that a lot of things could happen.

Even after the surgery was over, its mechanics remained abstract, at least as presented by my doctor. I was unable to process the good news that, except for the business of being sliced open and rearranged inside, I should expect a full recovery.

During a post-op visit, my doctor talked of wanting to quit being a surgeon to become a screenwriter—a bit of personal intrigue that, THANK GOD, he did not reveal until I was in the ICU and hopped up on morphine. Later, he would tell me the story. While sworn to secrecy, I can reveal that it sounded intriguing.

I was given excellent odds, not at all supported by information available online, percentages about recurrence that in my head made themselves into pie charts, evenly split. Against character, I remained inappropriately positive. My husband took our daughter to ski team training and races, tuned her skis, and took videos for me. My friends stopped by, but never on powder days, which was fine, since I didn't want to hear how great the snow was. At home, I tried to read, but could not concentrate. I survived on broth and *CSI* reruns.

Eight weeks and one day after my Christmas-eve surgical event came an epic snowfall. Pristine, brilliant, and white beyond white, the morning cruelly teased my sensibilities, my "mind of winter," as Wallace Stevens said.

By four in the afternoon the day before, the schools were ordered closed for the next day, not so much because the roads would be impassable, as we all had high-clearance trucks, but because no one would have shown up. This spectacle unfolded through a prism of icicles, some up to three feet long, which hung outside the window in my living room, where I was two months into my three-month sentence of couch arrest. I watched the storm warnings out of Albuquerque until I could no more. My daughter said she hoped the snow would be too deep for practice, wishing for a "free day" to just be a kid in the fresh powder.

I had gone back into the hospital several times since December. Violently allergic to the pre-surgical antibiotics—code for: they wouldn't stay in me—I caught one infection after another, some interesting, the others dangerous. Whatever part of my body was supposed to take nutrients from the food I ate had declined to do so. Despite this, I was told that my recovery, from a surgical standpoint, was ahead of schedule. I would not be tested again until May, so missing this snow, on this day, would have no relationship to my prognosis. It was more about the fact that I could barely stand up.

Compared to being trapped in my house, the physical discomforts were minor inconveniences. I slept ten, sometimes twelve, hours a night, just to pass the time. Noises had been made that perhaps I needed antidepressants, which I resisted. The crisis, as I saw it, was this snow already piled three feet deep and so white that it was baby blue. The dagger was knowing this much powder at the 8,000-foot elevation where I lived equaled five feet, even six, up on the mountain.

I got my ski pants out of the back room, just to look at them. My favorite pair was brown plaid with lots of pockets, including an insulated one for a phone, so that the battery holds all day. Such considered design! It also had a series of grommets to run a headphone cord up the side of the pant, but I'd never gotten the coat that went with. I put them on, just to see, over one of the pairs of long underwear that had been my daywear for the last few months, the waistband rolled down so that there was no pressure on the scar. Those pants fell right down to my knees. I'd lost as much weight as my visitors' expressions had indicated. Even after I put on my specially ordered extra-small truss, those pants weren't staying up. I found an old pair of my daughter's suspendered, race-training ones, the kind that usually go over a speed suit and can be removed while still in one's skis, tear-away style—another fine piece of engineering. I filled up the space where the muscles should have been with extra layers. I couldn't help but hope that—no matter how diminished my body had become—it might still remember.

My plan was to drive up the mountain, certain that getting out of the house could only be beneficial—despite my involuntary driving hiatus. I will confess that I put in my contacts. In my everyday life I prefer to wear glasses, but they don't fit under my goggles. Even the most half-assed investigator would have known that something self-delusional was afoot. I also picked up my ski mittens, which I can't wear to drive because they are like teddy bear paws. So, there was evidence, absolutely. But the story I was telling myself was about a quick visit and looking. Only looking.

The trip up the hill was one of the first times I'd been in my truck since the surgery. Just being in it, making my way up the twisty road, felt like a part of myself was returning. The road, the falling rock warnings, the sheeted rivulet alongside—everything was as it had always been, as I would soon be, as well.

In the parking lot at the resort, the excitement was palpable. The lot wasn't that big, a person could easily walk in, but I took a shuttle, to best save what little energy I had. From the bus, I could see that the front face of the hill didn't look crowded. Locals always head to the back or the ridge, hoping to make fresh tracks. Not my concern, I told myself. I was just up for a peek.

I thought I ought to take a look in my locker and make sure my stuff was still there. I could have been evicted or something for having gone missing for so long. I'd check on my gear, get a fancy coffee, and sit with the snow bunnies at the picnic table at the base of Al's Run. Then I'd go home.

I was comforted by locker room three's specific

aroma: sweat, wet wool, and chocolate—the smell wafting from the candy store, which makes their hot chocolate old-school: milk and actual chocolate with chili powder, the New Mexico way.

Getting my ski boots on was something of a challenge. The bones in my feet had relaxed, what with all the couch-sitting I'd done. I couldn't fold into that half-stand-half-crouch position that gives a person the angle to slide into a boot engineered to be tight enough to keep the foot from torqueing on impact. The process, which included flopping down on a bench for a rest, took what felt like an hour. Other skiers came and went, commenting on my absence (about which I was vague), and welcomed me back.

When I climbed up the cleated steel stairs to the base, a bizarre rush of something replaced the malaise I'd been dragging around. Even now, I can't find the words for it. Perhaps one might be conjured: at-home-ness? My body had memorized this place: the combination to the locker room, the way I have to stand on tip toes to get my boots down from on top of the cabinet, how to talk on a cell phone hands-free by tucking it between the ear pads in my helmet. I clipped into my skis, calling up the muscle memory I'd need to move about encumbered by five-foot-long planks.

The glide over to the lift, only about twenty-five yards, caused me no pain, or none that I remember. Someone slipped in behind me in the queue. I could have ducked under the rope and made my retreat, but I never considered it.

When the attendant scanned my pass, the date of its last use flashed on his monitor. "Where have you been?" the dude said. "Jail or something?"

I tried to chuckle back, but I bet I just grimaced.

The glint off of the mountain was blinding. I had not seen light this bright for many weeks.

I rode up with my friend Jack, who had taken in my husband and daughter for Christmas dinner while I was in the ICU alone and not knowing to press the button for more pain meds. I had sort of hoped to not run into anyone who specifically knew I was supposed to be doing the opposite of getting on a ski lift. Our daughters, who were in the same classes in middle school, raced alpine together. Both girls were excellent students but hell-bent on focusing their energies on racing down icy courses at speeds nearing sixty miles an hour. There was no competing with the thrill. Jack set gates, and I refereed, and as such, we had done this ride up the lift many times at sunrise to prep for a race. Our hill is at its most beautiful at dawn, even when it's fifteen below.

Jack's wife was a medic for the team, and my husband filmed their runs. The two of them had first-hand knowledge of the gnarlier wipeouts, whereas Jack and I got our news by way of the coaches' gasps on our single-channel radios. We all prayed that these girls would get over it before suffering a debilitating crash or missing so much school while on the road with the team that they lost their chances for the top-tier colleges for which we'd preferred they'd be gunning. Our girls are of this place, and there's nothing to be done about it.

At the top of the lift, as I readied to slide onto the landing, I thought: Now here's a moment when this adventure of mine could go very wrong. It had only been two months, yet I wondered what muscle memory, if any, had survived. I had straitjacketed my midsection into submission; this day would be, by default, all about my thighs. I knew Jack would sweep me out of the way of the chair if I stumbled. He understood why I was there, knowing that I ought to have been on my couch. He would neither admonish me if this went poorly, nor congratulate me if it ended well.

"You good?" Jack said. "Snowmobile ride back down if you want. No questions." He asked this not because he thought I would take him up on the offer but because he knew a potential disaster when he was sitting next to one.

I told him I'd make my way around the back of the hill, staying on easy greens, nice and slow. My reasoning for not skiing down the front of the hill that day was supposedly because it was too public; in reality, it's because it was too bumpy. Instead, I took a flat run, barely a slope, over to the lift that would take me to the back side. I shied away from areas where there might be a hidden bump or a need to make a quick turn. I moved like I had never before put on a pair of skis. Or something else: I'd never even seen someone ski, and I was a Weeble weighted in all the wrong places. I suspected that if I fell, I didn't have the stomach muscles to get back up. All I was fit for was rolling. For an instant, or ten, I considered mountain lions and hypothermia.

I rode the second lift, an old-school, wooden one, with a guy from Texas who'd heard the outstanding weather report while at work in Dallas the morning before. He'd skipped out at lunch, driving through the night to be here, for this snow. He didn't make first tracks, but was ecstatic nonetheless. Because he was a stranger, I could give him my facts. The Texan and I skied the first curve, barely a turn. I was afraid to lean in and I knew I was sitting back, the opposite of what one should do. I righted myself with a jerk that felt like electricity. My center of gravity was nonexistent. For the first time in years, I'd need to concentrate and do the things that beginners are told to do to keep from falling. I lied to the Texan, telling him I felt great, just slow, and that he should go. He raced off, all powder and euphoria. The truss, too loose, slipped northward, binding my ribcage, making it difficult to draw a full breath.

The flat and wandering run around the back side is over four-and-a-half miles long. I had, in the past, bombed down it in twelve minutes. On this day, it took me almost two hours, quite a lot of alone time.

I passed the bend where the previous December my cell phone half-rang and then disconnected because of the terrain. The message on my voicemail said that my mentor in art school had passed away from the very same kind of cancer of which I might, in four years and ten months, be considered cured—or so said WebMD.com. I am lucky, extremely so. I know this every minute of every day. Yet, my stomach felt like I'd been lowered gut-side down onto a table saw, and I'd have preferred it didn't.

I continued. I meandered, moving so slowly that it could be called nothing else. The day was too stunning to look at head-on. Each contour was either absorbed below my knees, or it was not.

I checked out the entry to a little tree run I love, Arroyo Hano, a sort of play on words, a ditch of a run named after the resort founder's son. It's lovely in there, isolated enough that you'd never know there was a terrain park just on the other side. It has the charm of those small, triangular plops of public lawn you see in cities, with only one bench and always a plaque for some unfamous person who had loved that view.

I didn't dip in. There was no way I could risk slamming into a tree, but I loved seeing the entrance and its promise to be there for me later. It was nearly too much, being back there. But the day wasn't about hitting my favorite runs or catching new powder. It was about ingesting this place as if it were a tonic.

I had skied until just before my surgery. On my last day up, lightheaded and jittery from the several days of the liquids-only, intestine-cleaning diet, I stuck to groomers. Prophetic of nothing, but still clear in my mind, were two easy runs, wide-open and flat, that I took, oddly enough, with my doctor. I had, on one or all of our visits in his office, harassed him about living in a ski town and never having skied. And there he had been, in a brand-new ski outfit, a season pass attached to the jacket's zipper. He'd clomped up the stairs to the base lift, evoking both Frankenstein's monster and a toddler, and I'd followed, hoping he wouldn't tumble backwards. He wanted to show me his skills. That day in December, he had just completed his first set of lessons, and he wore the scared-witless glow that verified he was hooked.

He wasn't a bad skier, my doctor, but was a stiff and cautious one. That seemed appropriate, given his line of work. Relax, you can still saw people open if you've ripped your ACL, I thought but didn't say. He was too new to have developed any bad habits. I skied behind him, which he said made him nervous. He would have been less pleased if I passed him and then forgot he was back there trying to recall if he should press on the uphill or downhill ski to make a turn. He had that look, the one that said he knew that some magic was waiting for him but that it would take patience.

When we took those two little runs, we did not once mention the surgery, then less than forty-eight hours away. On the lift, he told me what he'd done in his class, and I listened as if I didn't already know what went on, as if the miracle of pressing down on a ski's edge was a revelation to me as well. There had been a shift in power, or knowledge or something like that. He had his shelf of leather-bound books, and I had my eight-year-old scuffed boots, the warped closures held together with duct tape.

But this day's run was a different thing altogether. It was about reclaiming my own body, which I had so easily turned over to others. It was about a shift in trust—how the day would go down was entirely on me. I found unmarked snow on a gentle glade connecting two open spaces. No one was back there. The pass was too flat to interest experienced skiers—everyone local was up on the ridge. In summer, this is a good hike-to picnic spot, level enough to spread out a towel and take a nap. I pushed my way through, knees bent, butt out, as if ready to sit. This trail is one that, in other years, I'd zipped through, as it's the shortcut around the back side.

My surgery had given me the gift of slowness and the time to pay attention. It was simply me, some big animal tracks, and the muffled grumble of a lift motor. The day had the best features of sugar, diamonds, and clouds, all merged into one—the sparkling negating the feeling that if I dared unzip my jacket, I might see what was left of my insides.

I'd bet that I was the slowest one on the hill that day. I suspect that I laughed or maybe screamed. Something loud came out of me, that much I recall. The sound announced something that was spring-loaded, from deep in my gut, where it had been lying in wait.

Snowfall was a relief, a bit of temporary magic.

We were born for the cold, the kind of kids who have one thing on their Santa list: a blizzard. We were a fungible group, my brother, random kids from around, whoever wasn't grounded or running a fever over 101 degrees.

We lumbered toward the outer reaches of parent-approved wandering, throwing hunks of ice at frozen apples. Pushing and pulling the shorter ones over a disused cattle fence, we plopped in heaps on the other side. We pretended we were the von Trapps sneaking over the Alps, hoarding snacks in our pockets in case they were our last.

We passed the convent's crumbling belfry and collectively sighed in relief. Our sounds ricocheted off the low walls that had been there since our parents were kids in the snow. Despite the rules, the rumors, the terrors, we were there for the sledding. We paused to admire three sets of fresh deer tracks, sneaking behind bushes whose Christmas-red berries, in a less exciting season, had sent two of us for a stomach pumping. We rounded the fishpond that was deeper than a man with his arms held up, or so went the lore. Filled with algae, semi-frozen but still smelly, this pond may or may not have taken the life of a six-year-old girl, *who was not Catholic*, the nuns had whispered. We flattened ourselves against the frosty wall. The chapel—pigeon-colored with a lot of points and edges—called to mind a medieval palace. We wished there were a moat.

A quick scoot across an open field, around a line of pine trees planted as a windbreak, and we were atop a pristine hill. On this morning, or some other: a broken nose, snow pants ripped apart by the blade on a flexible flyer, my brother crying. On that day, on all of them, we walked inside a snow globe. We stayed outside as our shadows lengthened in the setting sun, reluctant to surrender the freedom of the day.

THE TIDES WERE WITHIN HIM

The seaplane's growl had come from beyond the boat docked across from Ernie's, out over deeper water. Even before he saw it, before he grabbed his breakfast, before he even had time to pull on his shorts and brush his teeth, the whirr of the motor was in his nerve endings. It may have begun doing its work while he slept. It had been Ernie's favorite kind of night: a summer storm moving in as he was settling into his bed, the squall strong enough to rock him to sleep but not so aggressive that he needed to go check below deck for leaks.

But this was Ernie's morning, and he had scheduled himself some relax time, so relax he would. He collected his toast, daily banana, and a bottle of orange juice and climbed to his station on the roof. The webbing on his lounger was frayed, and at some point the seat would give way, but as it had the shape of his backside sunken-in just so, he couldn't think of replacing it. He had the crossword, a pencil, plus another for when that first one rolled away. He tipped his face toward the sun. Perfection.

When the plane appeared, Ernie tracked it as it dipped, moving in and out of the glare and buzzing the boats. When it levelled out, he shielded his eyes, hoping to get a good look. The pilot's shoulders were clenched toward his ears, his arms rigid. The word around the marina was that the plane seen hobbling around the bay on weekends was some rich guy's latest toy. His piloting skills were not increasing with practice, having plateaued right around medium-dangerous. Typical. Probably wearing crocodile loafers without socks. And a spray-on tan. Ramped up with designer coffee. To be clear, the two men had never met. The *pilot*—and around that word Ernie would have made air quotes, if he were that sort of a person—stood for everything negative ever said about Marin County. Despite not being from here, Ernie had taken a protective stance towards his newish home, particularly the waterfront— the *real* waterfront, meaning not just something pretty to fly over, badly, in a private plane. And, if this piece of work was the right guy, it meant Ernie's ex, Cindy, had picked *him* of all people for the upgrade. This spectacle of a man.

The docks were like blocks of apartment buildings set on their sides, with the skyward edges sliced off and set afloat. The dank of a few tons of wet cement saturated the salt air. TJ, the harbormaster, and a small, under-the-table crew were lowering a boat into its new barge frame, where it would be forever gripped, once the cement set up. Ernie had wanted to man the crane, but TJ's "Are you out of your mind?" put an end to that. It amazed and pleased Ernie that this was the surest way to support the tonnage. He felt sorry for the boats, demotored and trapped, but it was the only way to get insurance, which the marina now required. In the seventies, you could stick a tree house on a couple of homemade pontoons and they'd rent you a berth. "Back in the day," the old-timers said, climbing rope ladders onto their pirate ships.

Ernie considered the sun's location, guessing at the time. He'd have to leave early for work, as it was the Fourth of July and the traffic along the waterfront would be awful.

TJ was down on the main dock looping marine rope elbow to hand. Setting a barge was a whole lot of waiting, with brief intervals of level-checking and guy-wire adjusting.

"Know who that is?" Ernie asked, tipping his head towards the bay.

"Nope, but he's sometimes got a chick to ride along," said TJ, using the side of his foot to sweep a few stray mussel shells back into the water.

"Cindy," Ernie said, as if he knew for sure. He'd been regularly updating TJ on his Cindy-sightings since the breakup, but TJ did not seem at all intrigued by the intel.

"I don't know," TJ said. "She always seems so antsy. Like she has somewhere else to be. Looking for some better thing." This was a lot, coming from a guy who was such a stoic, whose usual response to any kind of drama, personal or water-based, was "use your head, man."

Cindy exuded self-confidence with such brilliance that its tentacles had wrapped around Ernie. But it wasn't all looks. Ernie loved the way she listened to him talk of his job, the weather, extreme high tide, whatever. That was in the beginning, of course.

"You on the weekend?" TJ said, instead of "Move on, man" or "Wake up already, she's a shrew." He and Ernie had been friends forever, but TJ couldn't relate to Ernie's continuing anguish.

"It's going to be nuts," Ernie said. "Good for tips, though."

Ernie had started finding his way to the sea decades before. Born into the high desert mountains, with their dust devils in spring, whiteouts in winter, summer monsoons, and virtually no autumn, he'd always felt he'd been meant for a different geography. While other kids analyzed incoming clouds for chances of snow, he pictured himself using a sextant to guide his crew home. It was never about beauty or freedom. He felt it in his body, in its chemistry. His inner ears sensed that there was too much gravity, and the horizon seemed too definite. He wanted a landscape with softer edges. He made a plan, which he kept.

Once he was old enough, he'd hitched to Albuquerque to take scuba lessons. The class was taught in a pool at the Y, but floating on his back, eyes shut, arms wide, he knew he was halfway home. It was strange to think about the sea in this overchlorinated pool in landlocked New Mexico. Ernie hadn't ever smelled salt air, yet he hungered for it. The sound of his breath on his first descent, the weight belts and respirator, the math of it all, was pure wonder. They took their final test in a quarry, the from-here kids laughing at them from the shore. The instructor, a former Navy Seal, told the group they were lucky to be taking the test here, away from "real water," where lots of folks get seasick when doing their first descents. Ernie wanted even that, to know the unease, stomach-lurching and wild. Ernie wondered if he suffered land sickness, if that was even a thing. On the way back to town, the instructor told them stories from his time in the service—he might as well have dropped Ernie at the recruitment office.

After he left the Navy, Ernie had gotten a job running day trips, mostly booze cruises, weddings, and corporate events, out through the Golden Gate Bridge. These jaunts on the *Selene* were only four to five hours, but this gave him enough time on the water to placate his system. He was still a captain, which sounded like more than it was. The people that owned the cruise company liked him to wear his officer's jacket, the white dress one, into which his slim torso still nicely fit. On the sunset tours, particularly the Singles-Mingle ones featuring a light-up champagne fountain, women would caress his epaulets with their manicured fingertips.

He had bought his current houseboat from an estate; he thought it might be fun, and if not that, interesting, to fix up and resell. It had the spine of something once beautiful. The previous owners clearly had a fondness for woodworking and stained glass, circa 1975. There was a mosaic of a topless mermaid in the shower stall that scared Ernie every time he walked into the tiny bathroom. It would take a lot of prying with a crowbar, maybe even some jackhammering, to get that thing out. Ernie tried not to think about what could lie underneath. The boat was named *The Rockhound*, which made sense after he learned that the former owners were geologists, but it also reminded him of digging around in the hard ground as a kid, checking every sharp piece of rock he found, hoping for an arrowhead. And then, of the way even the most mundane shards he collected seemed that much more special once the dirt was washed off and they lay glistening in a puddle of water in his palm.

No matter how many times Ernie retied the lines, his home rested at one and one-half degrees off level. Not much to the eye, but every time he dropped one of those stress balls TJ's wife had given him, it took off for the front door. Still, through the water stains and hints of black mold seeped definite evidence of love. For a while, the boat had lived under a tarp in drydock, the way other guys' 1967 Mustangs sat in their driveways. Then Ernie had cause to make it his home.

Ernie checked the time, gulped his juice, folded up the crossword, and picked up his banana peel. He'd been sitting outside longer than he'd thought, figured he should get ready for work. Overhead, the plane wobbled and dipped to within three feet of the water. The pilot hesitated and jerked it upward. He was so close to TJ's boat that the racket the props made seemed to bounce along the water. Ernie wondered if the dope had good insurance.

"Welp, work beckons," Ernie said to TJ, while still looking at the sky.

"I'll be the one called to pull that blockhead out of the drink," TJ said. "Just you watch."

Can't not land forever, Ernie thought. Sure hope I'm here to see you run out of fuel.

The plane arced a tight circle, angled down and touched the water, finally bumping to a landing, the kind that makes a person feel it in the gut, even if they're merely a witness. On this last pass, Ernie thought he might have seen the top of Cindy's blond head. Or a splash of light bouncing off the windshield. She had become a mirage, shinier and newer than the real thing.

"Did you see a passenger?" Ernie asked.

"I hate Fourth of July," TJ said, and headed back to his boat.

A holiday weekend paired with clear weather meant Richardson Bay would be gridlocked with sailboats and jet skis. People with the least bit of sense stayed off the water when it was this crowded, unless it was their job to be there. As tends to happen on any given summer weekend, regardless of visibility, the excursions for that night were sold out.

"Sorry, I can't," Ernie had said to the ticket agent who wanted to know if he couldn't place a few last-minute reservations. "Look, I'm maxed at ninety-five, that's it." Fog City was outsourcing its bookings these days—everyone was. Someone far away in a sweaty city who hadn't smelt the brine at low tide couldn't be expected to know the number of passengers tops out at the number of life vests.

When Ernie and Cindy first met, he was living on a different houseboat, one with an oven big enough for a turkey and a brushed steel refrigerator, albeit a galley-sized one. That boat had a built-in dehumidifying system that dumped the collected moisture back into the bay, which then evaporated into the air or gently pillowed into an early-morning mist. It had been a modern boat, with a formal hull, and didn't rock much at all—sometimes it hadn't even felt like it was on the water. If it wasn't for the moisture in the air and the occasional foghorn, he could have been anywhere—even back on the mesa, which had its own kind of stillness. To even detect movement, Ernie had to look outside through the efficient double-glazed windows and compare the roofline of the neighbor's boat to his windowsill.

Cindy had liked the idea of the boat, but this was before she realized it wasn't just a weekend thing. She had not been invigorated by the breathing-in of sea air. The ducks perched on the mangled aluminum chair protruding from the low-tide mud failed to charm. "People live this way?" she had said after the first night they stayed at his place rather than hers.

"Hundreds of them actually," Ernie said, his pride unable to overpower her shock. It was like they were breathing in different air. Cindy pointed out that the ramps squeaked at high tide, the windows were permanently etched into a haze by the salt and wind, and the docks were covered with shells discarded by the gulls. Ernie had never noticed any of these features, but once brought to his attention, they made him love the place more.

Despite these differences, they became a thing. After what would best be called a whirlwind courtship—*I'm in love!* Ernie had announced to TJ after a mere three dates—Cindy gave up her month-to-month lease (studio apartment, no view) and moved onto the houseboat. Following what Ernie considered an insufficient trial period, she had made the move to land a condition of their continued coupledom, claiming she couldn't stand the motion, the dampness, and the constant smell of decaying fish.

"I think there's mold," she had said after being away at her mother's.

"I doubt it. Maybe just low-tide smells," Ernie said.

"Well, whatever it is, it's more noticeable after being gone."

"Then don't go," he said.

Ernie thought a trip out of town might be good for them both. A couple's vacation, romantic, somewhere warm. Maybe an island where they could snorkel and Ernie could renew his scuba license. Cindy could get one or two of those flowery dresses ladies wore when they visited the tropics, and they could both enjoy cocktails decorated with skewers of fruit. Cindy was unenthused about the crystal blue waters and swaying palms as marketed by Ernie.

"I don't know why you never take me to the desert," Cindy said. One of her yoga friends had told her that it was magical, all that open space, and that there was an energy vortex. He'd heard that, for sure, but definitely not from anyone who wasn't just passing through. By this time, he had no people back there, but he agreed to go to a spa that Cindy insisted was supposed to be transformative. Life-changing.

He worked hard to avoid running into anyone he might have known back in the day, as the place had always been wall-to-wall "cousins," which just meant folks who knew him back when. He had to keep telling Cindy to drink more water, but she didn't and got a bit of the altitude. He tried to see the place with fresh eyes, but it didn't work. When she marveled at the curves of the old adobes, he saw what a man's hands looked like after a day of mudding, how there wasn't enough aloe in the world to relieve that kind of dryness.

"Welcome to the land of enchantment," their waiter said as the dreamcatchers in the window shuddered from the breeze. Is it your first time here?" Cindy ordered her enchiladas mild with the chile on the side.

"Christmas," said Ernie, hoping his chile order

would confirm him as homegrown. He heard his cadence come back, those pauses that tourists thought marked dim-wittedness rather than thought. He remembered what it was like to work service jobs that required a certain façade, to avoid flinching when he was asked, *Do you speak English?*

In the end, Ernie didn't think either of them did any transforming. While he felt she was daring him to not love the place that raised him, he felt oddly defensive of it and irritated that she had no interest in the "real" Southwest, how people lived there. But maybe time and distance had softened him a bit. The light *was* incredible, and the sunsets were more colorful than he remembered. If only she hadn't been so enamored with the "magic" of it all.

When they returned to California, Ernie agreed to try living on shore. Turned out, Cindy had been scouring the listings, had already found a rental property. Had boxes ready to go. Ernie stood by as the realtor pointed down the hill at the harbor. His harbor. "Whole lot of crazy going on down there," she said to Cindy, handing her both sets of keys.

"You don't even know," said Cindy. "Moving on up, as they say." To Ernie, being so high up over the water and yet the ground feeling so solid—it was strange. Cindy pointed to the rental truck, his cue to start unloading. He couldn't wait for the fog to roll in.

They moved into the small house on the hill, so far up that its eaves rested in fog. Cindy bought Ernie a rusted anchor to put in the front yard. They painted the house blue and gave it a name, like a boat: *Aphrodite*. Ernie had thought he could become happy, or at least content.

The stasis up there messed with his equilibrium; he developed reverse seasickness. Three months into the land-based experiment, he still swayed, his sea-legs stationed at wider than hips-width apart as he tried to steady himself against the earth's lack of movement. The gentle rocking had been in his nerve endings for too long.

Cindy swore Ernie swooped sideways at times when he should have been still. She'd place her hands on his shoulders and press down, hoping to make his body realize it rested on solid ground. "Stop moving. You're driving me nuts," she had said, at first joking, and later, not.

Without the change of tide, he was always off: early to the dentist's, late to work. He felt nauseous in their house, so he took to wearing sea-bands while on land, which caused people to stare at his wrists. When he did take them off, the metal disc that was supposed to affect a pressure point left a little divot.

One day, trying to get a feel for how high up they were, and how far from the bay, Ernie had balanced sock-footed on the edge of the bathtub and craned his neck. Hands on the windowsill, peering between the trees, he could see a thin strip of water, where the bay met the craggy shore of Tiburon. Cindy stood in the doorway, shaking her head. She let out an aggressive sigh, not even glancing towards the sea.

"Just looking," Ernie had said, but she had already left the room.

When he couldn't sleep in the blue house, Ernie had stealthed out to the cruise ship. He'd lie on the deck with his arms and legs splayed, face to the sky, drinking in the moist air. He'd wake up to the seagulls and the foghorns, feeling rested, his clothes soggy from the mist. Eventually, he was sleeping more often on the roof of the ship than in bed with Cindy.

"Why can't you just have an affair, like a normal person?" she had said.

While he was packing, Cindy told Ernie that he had been interesting, *on paper*. By then, they were at the point where she didn't care enough to engage in a good fight and he was too exhausted by his own ennui to mount a decent defense.

Ernie had been good on paper and still was. In a self-directed pep talk, he enumerated his bonus points while getting ready for work, thinking perhaps this would be the evening he met a woman so singular she'd cancel out his longings for Cindy. He had a job, hair, and all of his teeth. He was in reasonably good shape—it does take decent leg strength to keep balanced upon the waves. He was the right amount of amusing when he's had a couple of drinks, and knew to keep it to a few. He had that boat, which gathered him a bucket of marketability points when said the right way. Granted, he lived on it, but the ladies never seemed to listen to that part. In addition to the white one, he had a blue suit jacket with an array of medals and brass buttons. The color highlighted his eyes, or so he had been told; he wore it with white creased trousers and deck shoes.

After work, when emptying his pockets, he often discovered neatly folded slips of paper upon which women had written their names and phone numbers. Sometimes the messages included a brief description to refresh his memory, as if *he* was the one who'd had four sloe gin fizzes. He never called these numbers, but neither did he throw out the pieces of paper, which tended to be cocktail napkins or the corners of free tourist maps from the kiosk near where the ship docked. At the end of the day, he would unfold the scraps, flatten the creases with a fingernail and stack them in a wooden box with scrimshaw of a whale on the top. It had been Cindy's gift to him their first Christmas together. The box opened with a tug and a squeak, the wood swollen from the damp. Some things can't be forced from their true nature, from their landscapes. But with the gift, Ernie realized later, maybe Cindy was trying. While it was about the sea, that box wasn't meant to live on the water. The inside smelled of cedar, as did the notes.

When Ernie moved back to the marina, he took up residence on the fixer houseboat and rechristened her *Thetus*. He and TJ lowered her back into the water with a boat hoist, two slings, and a prayer. The slip he took faced inward, towards the land and the hill and his former house. He was across from the harbormaster's rigs, a barge outfitted with a crane, a pile driver, several generators, welding equipment, and a giant magnet—a view that pleased him. The magnet came into play when Ernie's Hibachi slid off his back deck. He'd always thought the magnet was a joke, just as TJ thought someone losing a 30-pound grill had to be. "You of all people should know that if it's not tied down, it's going over," TJ said.

The storm the night before had a lot of muscle, though the morning's bluebird sky denied it. The weather had snuck up, winging anything in its path. Life vests casually tossed aside took flight, kayaks freed themselves; there was even a rumor that someone's dog—taken to sleeping nights on the roof deck—had been sucked out to sea. One boat had a cement brick go through its skylight and land on the couch.

"Anyone who leaves crap like that on their roof doesn't deserve skylights," TJ said. As much as TJ groused about folks not using their brains and not knowing how to tie a decent knot, he was the go-to guy when things went wobbly in a storm, or a king tide was due to strike. He just did not want to have to talk about anyone's love life.

Ernie had thought his split with Cindy was amicable, but word of his moodiness and late-night disappearances funneled their way back to him, made *him* sound like the unreasonable one. When they did run into each other, he worked on appearing to be friends and had almost convinced himself that they were. A few weeks back, at the farmer's market, Ernie attempted to be casual, tossing an organic artichoke from one hand to another. When they had been together, other men's stares had both unnerved and pleased him. And here he was, rather ruffled himself. Whatever attracted him in the first place was still there. What was it—her confidence? It was the way she seemed so sure of her place in the world, something Ernie envied, despite his having found his way to what felt was his real home.

"You look well," Ernie had said. "Content. Rested." Some small talk, as TJ's wife had advised. Nothing too needy.

"You know, I've met someone," Cindy said. "You may have heard. We've gone to Santa Fe twice."

"Good for you," said Ernie, dropping the artichoke on her foot.

She'd spoken of the friend's successful business as a motivational speaker, his artistically designed and mammoth house, and his new plane. "Just a hobby," she'd said, the *as it should be* implied.

"Come by the marina sometime," he had told the back of her as she walked away.

Ernie decided to go with his captainly white jacket for the holiday. It set off his *legitimate* tan, as he saw it, and made him look like a man of the sea. He carried it to work hung in a plastic drycleaner's bag to keep it pressed and safe from seagull droppings.

"It's a great day to be out on the water," he told the passengers, many in patriotic and nautical get-ups—the captain hats, anchor-print skirts, American flag everything—as they shuffled onto the *Selene*. He said this to every group that boarded his ship, and not once did he have to lie. "Fireworks viewing should be superb," he said into the intercom while maneuvering the ship into traffic. The International Orange of the Golden Gate Bridge as contrasted against the deepening blue of the sky made Ernie woozy, it was so perfect. "Welcome to my excellent life," he said, forgetting to take his finger off the talk button on the speaker.

The passengers moved portside to look at the bridge. The shift in their weight tilted the boat and the coffee Ernie had left on his control board slid, spraying his trousers but somehow missing the jacket. He had taken to talking up the bridge, which, while a familiar vista to just about everyone, was in danger of being overshadowed by the flashy, new light show on the remodeled Bay Bridge. "It's like Vegas," Ernie said, taking anyone's admiration of the computerized effects as a personal affront.

Again came that seaplane, shaky as ever. Back for round two. It would be a thing to see fireworks from a plane, if a person liked fireworks and had a plane, that is. The plane crossed overhead and dropped suddenly, to about five feet above the water. Its tiny cockpit contained two people, a pilot and a female passenger, whose hair sure looked like Cindy's, or maybe a little blonder. She had the same way of talking with her hands waving about in front of her for emphasis. Ernie always liked the way she talked with her whole body. On one of their first dates, when she put her lovely hand on his forearm, he nearly passed out from the frisson. But now when she put her arm on the pilot's shoulder, Ernie shivered. They slid out of view, as if to taunt him. Funny how someone who had said she had a problem with too much movement ended up in a seaplane with this knucklehead.

As the plane moved away, Ernie underwent his own distancing. He felt it bodily—whatever he had in him that longed for Cindy sluiced out of him and into the night air. Not a revelation so much as a recognition. They both had what they wanted now: he had the sea, and she had success, if vicarious. This, he believed, he could handle.

The pilot ascended again and veered towards the shore. The shallows were dotted with windsurfers, and the bulkhead was crowded with strollers and rental bikes. Aggressively vacationing, the masses chomped king crab leg cocktail on restaurant patios just feet from the water, shading the screens of their phones to look at the pictures they took of the bay with Alcatraz a hump in the distance.

The plane plopped down and out of Ernie's view. The maneuver was similar to the pilot's earlier attempts, except that this time he would have little leeway. A bit of wind had kicked up, pushing the surface of the water into gentle swells and a smattering of whitecaps.

The plane wove in and out of Ernie's line of vision, the hum of its engine fading and returning.

Soon enough it would be dusk, so Ernie would get a break from looking at and, he hoped, thinking about the pilot—unless this dope didn't know it was both impossible and illegal to land a plane on unlit water. The latter part of each cruise, when Ernie would turn off the lights in the pilothouse, the contours of the water crispening as his night vision kicked in—this was the splendor of the evening for him. If he got light in his eyes from, say, the fantasia that the Bay Bridge now was, even the flash of a camera—and especially the fireworks— it would be a good fifteen minutes until he could see again. He liked to think that the contraction of his pupils, rather than being pure biology, was some sort of psychological response to the intrusion into his night.

On their final descent, Ernie got such a good view of them, Cindy with her wacked-out hair, a weird yellow color that reminded Ernie of a newborn chick, and that what's-his-name—so close Ernie could see his hair plugs. No, that part's a lie, but he could imagine it.

As the plane lowered to just a few feet over the water, a jet ski crossed in front. The plane dipped and dipped, and the jet ski's wake lifted and lifted and caught the plane's nose and yanked it, put it in a headlock. The skier looked back as the plane took a few terminal skips across the skin of the water. He smiled or grimaced; it was hard to tell. There were several metal-to-water bumps, sort of a crack and a hollow thump at once. Ernie felt it in his spine, the crumpling, and wondered how much stress would finally make it crack.

Ernie saw this was a mission to be made solo—a toss-up between whether he meant to only take a little look or to go all Samaritan. The cruise ship was a barge, only about six feet under the surface of the water, so Ernie could pull in close to the shallows where the plane had crashed. He told his chief mate, who was already stunned that they had turned towards land, to take over in the pilothouse. He then went to the lower deck and untethered one of the fiberglass capsules that contained an inflatable rescue raft. He took off his shoes. He was all about protocol, except that part about unleashing a raft and abandoning ship. He clipped on a painter line and released the capsule. Once he pulled the cord, the CO_2 inflated the raft in what felt to Ernie like super-slow motion, although he knew it to be only about fifteen seconds. A crowd gathered at the railing, sure they were about to collect an awesome vacation story.

The tide was running in Ernie's favor, the wind at his back. He felt like he was acting out the modernization of a Greek tale he'd half-learned in middle school. If this act of heroism (or extreme foolishness) didn't show Cindy that he was worthy, capable, and deserving—well, Ernie didn't consider for a moment that it wouldn't. Ernie wouldn't have minded being called chivalrous, but mostly he wanted to cause Cindy to feel regretful. That *he* might be the one who got away. He gave the line a few tugs, to be sure that he wasn't going to be pulled out to sea.

Cindy and her guy were just waiting there, the seaplane adrift and floating, exactly like it's supposed to. Cindy sat on the edge of the cockpit, and the pilot messed with his phone. She half-waved, keeping her elbow at waist level. When the pilot glanced at her, she put her arm down by her side and looked away from Ernie, off towards the shore.

Ernie's raft bobbed away from the shore in the ebbing tide. He stretched out his legs, rested his head on the bumper, and let his hands fall into the water. He didn't even feel the raft moving but knew that it was. A person adrift at sea would die the same way someone lost in the desert world, he thought. Disoriented and thirsty. He closed his eyes against the sun and heard snippets of yelling from the shore as well as the idling motor of his own boat.

All along, Ernie had thought that the worst thing in the world would be to know what Cindy told her new beau about him. That he was a hobo or unhinged. That she had told him nothing was a dagger the sharpness of which he had not considered. He saw that neither he—nor their relationship—featured prominently in Cindy's story of her own life. How could he have missed how lopsided they'd been? He wished he could muster up some anger, but all he felt was hurt.

"Get over here already," the pilot said, like this had all been Ernie's fault. As if he had some right to boss Ernie around. Not so good with the motivational speech under pressure, this one. "Don't you know who I am?" the pilot said.

Someone from the harbor police or Coast Guard would turn up soon, *so just cool yourself down*, Ernie thought or perhaps said out loud. Maybe he even yelled it to the guy, who then gave him the finger, called him a dumbass, and threatened to sue. A news helicopter came in close and was hovering over the plane. Surely, they would call for help.

Cindy yelled his name, or so Ernie thought. It was hard to hear over the copter, but Ernie knew she recognized him, as well as the shift in dynamics. She waved her arms as if she were swatting at bees. Definitely not the SOS maneuver—both arms above the head in a Y—that Ernie had taught her. "Oh, you're fine?" Ernie said. "Great! Me, too. See you around then." He felt like this was some other guy acting and he was just a witness. It was not in his nature to leave someone in peril, but it felt great. What would Cindy say? *Empowered.*

Ernie turned towards the ship and motioned to a deckhand to reel him back in. The passengers, who just a few seconds ago had seemed eager to cheer, did not. Ernie ordered the chief mate to turn the boat, to make their way to deeper water to secure a view of the fireworks.

While Ernie was changing into dry clothes in the darkened pilothouse, the images fanned across the internet. They showed a guy in a life raft next to a seaplane, smiling like a lunatic. The late-day sun accented the contours of the plane's crumpled-in nose, which looked like an eggshell into which some giant had pushed his thumb. Ernie hadn't seen that part; it had been around the other side. Nor had he seen the plane sink or the tug that rescued them, helping them aboard from their perch on the wing just before it fell below the waterline. The plane's shiny, new interior would soon enough fill with ooze and suction itself to the shallows.

As always, the fireworks' grand finale felt never-ending. Particularly oppressive was that last part when the sky was filled with illuminated chrysanthemums—too much cheer for Ernie's liking. And the cacophony. He preferred the silence and the residual vapors that followed. There was a deliciousness to the absence, like a pressure drop or the ebb after a wave. A magic, even. Real magic.

In the morning, TJ would be summoned to drag the plane to drydock. While the job would be too much for the giant magnet, Ernie thought he'd like to go along, to help winch the sorry thing onto TJ's barge and watch the mud and seaweed flush out.

TUMBLE

Like little kids, we inventory our wounds, the injuries witnessed, and the slopeside hearsay. Everything is epic.

"Had to pop my own shoulder back in," we all say, eventually, in the bar, after a few.

"They went melon-sized," the medic says of our injured knees.

"I couldn't even find my second pole after," says any one of our kids to a friend, thinking we don't hear.

"My bindings are shot. Ripped right away from the base." Could be any of us, the way we behave.

We've never been risk-takers, not really, which isn't so much fueled by anxiety as it is by pragmatism. *We paid for this ski pass*, we reason, *so we aren't going to lose a season by being in a leg cast.* And yet, the rush.

It's late season, an afternoon of flat light—and

we're at the top of that hill that everyone dislikes, but this time, with ice. We're well into the thaw-freeze cycle, and the crusty pack glistens. A few head down, braking, then waving the rest of us to follow. It hasn't snowed in over a week and the moguls are deep and hard. Nasty.

Our hearts beat from the wrong place in our chests and the run feels like a thing to get over. A man from somewhere behind asks, "Are you going, or what?" Now it is a challenge for me alone, since the hill cares nothing about a group.

I click my poles together, and push off, but without confidence, without assessing the hill, and just like that, I'm flat on my back, my head, my fucking shoulder that hasn't been the same since the car accident in college or that try at rock-climbing or loading boxes into our storage unit—and now this.

How did this even happen? We usually can't tell, it goes down so fast. Technically, it was the sitting back. *Lean forward,* we've heard since forever, repeated it to our kids, who have dusted us, because this mountain raised them. They can get down this hill without thinking about it, even on a beast of a day such as this, because they are naturals.

And we are not.

I'm alert while tumbling, listening for snapping bones. I've somehow never even fractured anything and here I go, about to split my head open. I hear the crumbly grind of my helmet lumping its way down the hill, feel the strap choke my neck, holding that headgear on, just like it's supposed to. My skull bumping around like a superball and I think: *this is what a head injury is like.* My body slipping—finding gravity—with the top of me pointing down the hill. Something rips.

Everything about this is new.

It's a long hill. I do not want to be myself right now. It's impossible to picture what this looks like, and yet, I've witnessed it before. I see my favorite colors: green and white. Evergreen and crystal-colored—the trees, the snow flashing by—and fast. Except that I'm the thing with all the movement—at great speed but also trapped in slow motion, inside the action and above it. The sun is like a spotlight beaming through the trees, harsh and blinding.

One of us in the swirling distance yells.

I stop sliding, and the rest of us circle, looking down at me like I'm an exhibit or an unearthed corpse, blocking my view of the sky, saying things like, "Did anyone call the patrol?" And, "Should we move her?" We all picture the backboard that should be en route, its restraints flopped to the side, a warming blanket and a neck brace sitting on top. We have seen that sled towed by a patroller in a red rescue jacket, wondered about the person being swifted down the hill to the med center.

An X is made out of two ski poles jambed into the crusty cover, right at my feet, which are pointing up the hill. We know the danger of someone coming down too fast, those skinny sticking-up poles a premonition of a gravestone, not the warning they're supposed to be. One of them topples over and clatters further down the slope, sounding like a cheap toy. A single ski pole stuck in the ground has no meaning. It's just a thing to run into.

I get up. Dizzy but able to stand. I palm a hand across the dent in the back of my helmet and feel that it hasn't cracked. My ski pants tore, but not down to the skin.

I'm woozy, but not vomiting. My pupils are not dilated, or so I'm told. Someone laughs a bit, so I laugh. It probably was a sight: me rag-dolling down the hill. Happens all the time, in bigger and faster ways. No need to call for a sled.

So, we finish the day, taking the easiest route down. Unsupported, but slow. Ample time to assess: my bindings didn't pop like they should have. Some joker, maybe me, set the dins too high, which is why I ended up slidng head-first. Those skis were the thumping noise. The drag was why I couldn't self-arrest. That or I forgot to try. There were so many things to think about. It is hard to take a full breath, which could be nerves or a popped rib. Someone says "yard sale," and someone else says "sick." Someone says some nonsense about getting back on the horse, and someone else says something about disbelief and a back not snapping.

I may say I'll do the run again—someday—but what I'm thinking is, *never, never, never.*

Later, I watch with fascination as the bruises on my back go from fresh-red, to purple, then to a greenish-yellow color that stays for weeks. I get chiropracted and acupunctured.

I hold onto the single-crash helmet with the grapefruit-sized crater in the back, keeping the thing hanging in the laundry room next to the rack where the ski clothes dry. Memento or warning—could be both. Eventually, I'll circle the damage with a black marker and write *do not use* in angry letters and throw it in the trash. I should probably saw it in half so that none of the dumpster divers in town try to salvage it for resale.

One day, maybe, I'll look at that hill and not feel blood rushing in my ears, won't feel my back begin to sweat, won't grip my poles as if they'd hold me to the mountain. I'll stop avoiding the others because I don't want to have to say: *Anywhere but that hill.*

We've all done it, made that tumble. We tell our kids to keep an eye out for each other. We tell ourselves we're being prudent, *not getting any younger* and *old bones heal slow, we're having an off day,* whatever. For now, for a time, I'll take the easier, more circuitous route down, alone, pretending this is a choice.

Soon It Will Be Summer

You pretty much know when you hear the helicopter that it's about a back, neck, or skull. It was just after we opened full-up for the season, all the runs going, but before the Christmas tourists come in. There *has* to be a first big emergency of the winter, I mean, it's going to happen, but when it does, it's always a shock. When that air ambulance lowered, the prop's rush pushed snow off the trees like a giant vacuum in reverse. Everyone stopped skiing, as if it were a crime to move while the backboard was being loaded. As soon as the whirring faded, it was back to vacation mode.

After a not-so-decent amount of time, the tourists hunt down anyone in a uniform jacket. They interrogate us, getting off on being closer to danger than their back-home lives allowed. We hardly ever tell the truth, but it's good to have some kind of idea of what to lie off of.

"A kid, is what I heard," one of the lifties said. These guys, stuck at the base of the hill all day, were relay stations for slope-side gossip.

"Total yard sale in the glade," my buddy Slice said. "Little girl. Tiny."

"Neck? Lung?"

"Nope, but she was out when they found her. Taking her for a scan."

"From away?" the lifty asked.

"Nope. Here," Slice said. The lift op grabbed the back of the chair as it swung around, tilting it so that we couldn't sit down. "Dude. Come on. This is heavy." Slice and I were manhandling a four-foot-long roll of B-netting onto the chair. It weighed like eighty pounds and no good could come of us dropping it once we were in the air.

"She was there for don't know how long," I said. "All alone, face down in the snow. Now let up." When he released the seat, it got Slice and me in the back of the knees.

"We were all in there when we were that age," Slice said. But he meant my sister, Willow. She was the one who always slid first into a blind drop like she had nothing to lose. That moment when you crest the edge, your heart wedged in the back of your throat—that's what kept her going. This little girl had to be one of the kids that had watched Willow from the lift, wanting to grow up to be her. If her tiny body managed to make it, she'd grow her hair long and zip past the bigger kids screaming, *So long, suckers!*

"Hell, we were jumping down the chutes by that age," Slice said. "Today just wasn't her day."

"I guess," I said, not remembering much of anything from before my mom got sick. I was born about to be motherless. When I was losing her, I'd space out on the lifts, imagining what if I had a bad fall, like a neck snap. What my funeral would be like and whether they'd throw my ashes off the peak the way they've done for people who died up here. Mom didn't tell us what to do with hers. They were still in a Talavera vase in the bay window of the part of the trailer that used to be her studio. The same window where she had set apricot pits to dry in the sun.

I started at the bottom. Literally. That's the big joke all new hires have to hear. Whatever. You stand around at the base all day, scan people's lift tickets, help little kids onto the chair, take a quick look at people's equipment to be sure that there was nothing so janky that someone could get hurt. The lifties were all either kids just out of high school or injured ski patrollers. A few were instructors that they couldn't quite fire, usually for drinking or hitting on a bunny that turned out to be some realtor's wife number three. Pre-season, they put us to work setting hay bales on the ski cross course and the terrain park. Later, they'd become parts of humps and the arcs of high-walled turns. People think those contours are pure snow, but they're not. Plus, we picked up all the crap that people dropped off the lifts during the winter before. When the snow melts, it's like a big junk drawer under there: car keys, cellphones, retainers. And wallets with out-of-state licenses, condoms, sometimes a few bucks, which we called our tips.

The tourists say, *Heaven*, and I've got to agree.

When at seven a.m., we caught a few runs before work, we said, *this* is why we live here. First tracks on Tell Glade and I felt it in my thigh muscles, right above my kneecaps, towards the outside, that specific burn that comes only with plowing through three feet of fresh powder. Me with some buddies from the crew, sweating and freezing at the same time and feeling lucky to have this gig where we get paid way too little for the opportunity to stand outside in ten-degree weather, our hips permanently canted to the angle of the hill. This is where I lived, right below the tree line, waist-high in snow.

"It will be hard to leave," I said.

"You're so not going anywhere," Slice said, as he hop-turned and slid away.

Up at the patrol hut, there was this little boy getting his picture taken with the rescue dogs. "Yo, jump in," the handler said to Slice and me. We posed, Slice with his arm on the boy's shoulder. Part of the job was appearing as supporting cast members in other people's vacation shots. It was about our outfits, not us, but still, I was always stoked to see kids getting into the sport, even if they did more toppling than skiing.

"Smile, Todd," said the kid's dad. "So your mom sees you're having a good time."

"Hey little dude," Slice said to the kid, "Been ripping it up?" Slice fist-bumped him, and they both beamed. His vibing with the kids wasn't even part of work to him; it was in his wiring. The dad turned his back to his son and took a swig. You'd be surprised to see how many people keep a flask with them. Because skiing is so awful that they need to take the edge off and all.

The handler released the dogs, and they were all over Slice like he was their long-lost puppy-brother. "Hey Ez, there's a bunch of messages for you on the board," said the handler. "Tried to call you, but I couldn't get a channel."

Willow. Who else. The only other person who ever calls was right here rolling in the snow with the dogs.

"Your sister rang like every five minutes for the last hour," said my boss, Jan, as I opened the door to the hut. "Using some mighty tangy language. The last couple times she said to go to the birthing center."

Ahead of schedule.

"Film it, will you? It'll be awesome," Slice said. "I can make the soundtrack." Sure thing, Slice, that's going to happen. "Know what? I totally need to be there."

"You are going nowhere, my friend. You see how busy we are?" Jan said to Slice, and I was relieved a bit because while it would be nice to have someone else there, Slice wanted to film every damn thing, which was just weird. He was always making little ski videos, us doing tricks and such, and yes, he was like family, but still. A person has to draw a line. "I don't even want to let this one go, except I'm afraid of getting beat up by his sister." Jan poked me in the shoulder and said, "Be back tomorrow," like I was unreliable. And here I was the only guy who hadn't, even once, been so hung over that I had to hurl from the lift. Jan berated us some more, acting like we don't all know he was a racer on the way up until he got one too many intent-to-distributes and got booted from the team. He still has the massive thighs. His family owns the Suppenküche, which is just bread bowls and soup, for Christ's sake.

It'd been just Willow and myself, on our own for a long time now, and it had worked out fine. I was in school, had no problem getting A's, and then it turned out that I could graduate a full year early. Compressed my schedule, no lunch, no study hall, took summer classes. The guidance counselor just about hyperventilated when my scores came in. Without me asking, she found scholarships that I could get for being a suspected genius *and* an orphan. Like it was some kind of a jackpot. Willow's way out of high school was to just leave.

"Ezra, I may have identified funding," the counselor had said. "For you. For college, so you can get out of here. And not make the same mistakes—"

"Don't even. You just don't know," I said. "And, it's Ez." There she was, assuming the same things as everyone else: hippie parents passing their recklessness gene onto their kids, if only the cycle could be broken, et cetera, et cetera. Judging.

"Look. You're intelligent. So smart, and you've held down a job and completed high school in three years. Why not cash in on that?"

"What if I don't want to go to college?"

"What are you going to do, ski and wait tables all of your life?" she said. "People don't get nearly perfect scores on their SATs and just stay here."

I had already rounded the corner into the stairwell. "What's so wrong with here?" I said back at her. "*You're* here, aren't you?"

There was still plenty of screaming left to go by the time I got to the birthing place. At first, they weren't going to let me into the room at all. They didn't believe that the brother was supposed to be there. Well, *me neither* dude. The whole thing was really crazy. Willow went bionic. She had no voice by the time that baby finally slid out. Just about split her open, from what little I could stand to see. And the pushing! I totally spaced on all of the calming stuff I was supposed to say. Most of the time I couldn't bear to go down to the end of the bed and watch. So much liquid and gunk. At least I didn't pass out. I'll say this: they're not at all cute when they come out, more like miniature, wrinkly old men. If the nurse hadn't stuck a pink index card with her weight and length on it, you'd never have guessed that baby was a girl. That card also had the mini footprints they take right after the baby is born. All ten toes were represented, but the line for the father's name had been left blank.

I had to take a little walk after. All the stuff that comes out after did me in. I ran into Slice wandering around the hallway.

"Oh hey, I was just looking for the baby display case," he said.

"How did you get in here?" I asked. "I had to fight to get in and I'm supposed to be here."

"Employee back door," he said. "I know a guy."

"Are you here to see Willow or just some random newborns?" I asked.

"Can I go see her?"

"Of course not," I said. "But man, it was unreal."

"Hey, know what, that kid? From today? They put her in a coma."

"Induced?" I asked.

"Yeah, that. Brain's all puffed up," Slice said. "They sent her up to Denver."

"Whose is she?"

"Local. A cop's kid or a fireman's, can't remember which. They told us after last sweeps. Probably didn't want it to get out while anybody was still around," he said. "Anyhow, want to go look in the baby window?"

Willow and I, but mainly her, were two of the best free skiers in the area. She was awesome, the aesthetics of her whole thing. She's never had an injury. Barely ever stumbled. She did smoke when she was up there, but, even wasted, she dusted most of the mountain. Skied with older local guys, lots of them huge, well over six feet, and she just flew on by, despite the fact that she had no gravity at all. You knew her because she went without a jacket and left her hair free. "I like to feel the air moving past me," she'd say.

When we were asked about competing freestyle, Willow screamed at the coach and then me. I brought up the prizes we could get: jackets, boots, things we could sell or actually use. I could have stood a new pair of skis. I took a core shot two winters back; the crack was awful. I landed the jump, sure, but right on a rock. Those raggedy skis were more P-tex than base.

"It's not something you win," she said. "It's how you live!"

We both also go backcountry and got asked to help when that stupid boarder from away went off-trail and got lost in the woods. Numbskull could have died; it dipped to some twenty degrees below that night. They had helicopters from the state out. Still couldn't find him. So after dark, we, meaning Willow and I and some other locals, were asked to go back. *Off the record*, Search and Rescue kept saying. This was code for *Don't bother suing if you get hurt because we'll all swear that you were never here.* But still, no one deserves to freeze to death, even an idiot. We found him in about two hours with our headlamps. Jerk didn't even thank us. I was fifteen.

It's looking like Willow's powder days were over, at least for now.

The last time I talked to Willow before the baby came, we were screaming at each other. She had clamped a spotlight to the rainspout of our trailer and was out there in snow boots and an old ski jacket of mine over top of her bathrobe. She was all stomach. Her, chopping wood, tears streaming down her face. Stumps everywhere. I had heard about the hormones.

"Stop it! What are you, crazy?" I said. She looked like something out of Hillbilly-Child-Bride Magazine, which is probably what people thought anyway. "Didn't they say something about not lifting things in the having-a-baby class?"

"Like you care," she said, "It's going below tonight. Way below. Want the pipes to freeze?" She turned for another log and tilted it vertical with her foot. She was huge, bigger than I'd have thought a person that tiny could stretch to. That had to hurt, all that making space for another person, like a reverse corset. She grunted like a dude each time she pulled the axe up to her shoulder. "Where the fuck were you last night, huh? I had to go to baby class all by myself." She looked at me instead of the stump and her swing went all wonky. Took off a sliver of bark, which could as well have been her foot. "Drove your stupid truck that I can't reach the brake on hardly, and everyone's all: Where's Ezra? Like you're the one having a baby." She had snot all coming down her nose, and she didn't even wipe it away. Frozen air billowed out of both of our mouths. "Then this bitch tells me I should give the baby away. Where were you, huh? *Where were you* when she said that to me?"

"I was working extra," I said. "Got a problem with that? Unless you're going to push out a bag of gold along with that baby, money is something we need more of." I had crashed at the lodge after pulling another double, taking every extra hour they would give me. I was kind of doing that: being up there more than not, working, going to the bar with the guys, napping on random couches. "Who do you think is going to support you and this kid? Not the actual father, I guess—who could be *anyone!*" She stared at me, jutting her lower jaw forward like a dare. She didn't have to point out that she was calling in a debt.

"Give me the axe," I said. "Go on in. I'll bring some wood in a minute." I couldn't help but remember all the firewood she cut up, first for keeping Mom warm, and then, me. Her all twig-armed, pulling that axe up over her head, a little squeak from her as she let gravity take over. It took her twice as many chops back then as it did me now just to split a single log.

There was about three hours' worth of stumps out in the yard. They had been dumped in a heap, like out of the back of a truck. I had no idea where they came from. We'd bartered our cut permit to a guy who resold what he chopped to people with vacation homes. We'd gotten three dozen eggs and a promise for more.

Swinging that axe around, I felt the moisture rolling down my neck from under my hat, the ends of my hair crisping as it froze. All she had to do was say, *Hey, it's getting cold*, and I'd have made sure we had wood. There was plenty up on the hill from the trees that last spring's avalanche drug down. No big deal. All this drama was unnecessary.

Willow didn't bring me a drink or a sandwich, like she was intentionally forgetting I was out there in the middle of the night hacking wood after being outside hauling things in the snow all day. She was a wiggled shape through the plastic sheeting that we put up over the windows. As a kid, sleepless, I'd listen to it ripple in the wind and find it soothing. Really bad winters, the kind that seemed more frequent when I was little, we'd nail blankets up as well.

I cut a ridiculous amount of firewood, just to make her feel bad, except I'd bet she never thought about it. If only she'd been decent enough to just *ask*, rather than assuming I owed her. Which, of course, I did.

And that baby class was a horror show. Something subliminal might have made me forget, but I didn't plan on missing. But I'll say this: all the other men were the dads, or at least they thought they were. The girls who didn't have a guy there had their mothers or some friend that was female. Not their little brother. On the first night, without any warning at all, they show us this video where the woman is screaming and all this gunk that is not baby is there. It would have been a good thing to show kids so that they don't have sex, like the way they show that movie at Driver's Ed with all those corpses lying around.

I knew I'd call back those colleges I turned down, see who would give me another shot and let me start in the summer. Maybe only one of my lesser picks, some tiny school in the far North, filled with gentle hippies from the suburbs who romanticized the kind of life we have here. Kids who say things like *living off the land* the same way I'd said, *I'm getting the hell out of here.*

Babies' bellybuttons are horrible, rotting things that eventually just drop off. That sure is not something that you want to step on in the middle of the night in your bare feet. But she's cute and all. Passion's her name. Not something you hear every day. Or ever. Supposedly, in terms of how much babies can scream, she was average. When she wasn't yelping, she was sleeping. She got to looking more the way a baby should, but still a little funky. The baby nurse said, "Well, what do you think you'd look like if you were in a tank of water for nine months then got squeezed out of a little hole?" True that.

Three patrollers got injured pulling stumps when the tow chain broke. They went flying, one taking a jab right through the lung by a hacked-off branch. Because I don't come to work wasted, I got offered a promotion to fill in one of the shortages and was put on avalanche crew and Search and Rescue. This had always been a fantasy of mine, the way kids in flat places dream of being policemen or firefighters when they grow up. We have more avalanches than fires, if you don't count the people who try to heat their trailers by cranking up the oven and leaving the door open.

Turns out, the job's a lot of taking snow samples and making practice grids. We do get to ride the lift in the dark for predawn drills, which is excellent. The search dogs go up there with us, hopping on the lift like it's some old couch. We turn off our headlamps when we ride up, and there are a gazillion extra stars. When you get off at the top, the dogs will pull you by a ski pole, which is like grabbing the back of a moving car when you're on a skateboard, but probably safer.

I liked my new schedule: up at four a.m., on the hill by six, seeing the sun come up over the peak. Willow and I were hardly ever awake at the same time. I was having two different lives, each of which cut into the other. One was like living the dream of a never-ending crystalline winter, and the other was the nightmare where you have a very important puzzle to complete and you are handed a pile of clues written in a language that you can't read.

Then, a massive storm hit, and an overnight

shimmer covered the rutted roads, the busted trucks in people's front yards as well as the old trampoline, wheelbarrow, and random crap in ours. Seriously, if it snowed all year 'round, you'd never know what holes some of these places were. Then came a thirty-inch dump. The snow plowed to the side of the road up to the resort was piled higher than my truck, making the drive to work like the luge, but slow and uphill. You couldn't see anything but the way forward. I was tempted to drive up the bank, just to see what would happen. A car on its side and pointed down the hill was wedged right into the wall. Crazy what a little momentum will do. I slowed down to peek in and make sure there was no one inside. Happens all the time: you slide off the road, you get out, hitch back to town. That car will be there until spring, longer if the roof has collapsed. In the meanwhile, it's a better warning than any yellow-painted sign with a squiggle on it. Road May Be Icy. No kidding. Everyone here knows someone who has flipped on this route or at least skidded off into the ditch that runs alongside. "See," they say pulling the hair back from their forehead. "Right here. There's still glass in there. Want to feel?"

A few weeks back, Willow's girlies from her café job threw her a shower, and for that moment, with all the squealing and pastel wrapping paper floating around in our trailer, the future had felt, if not optimistic, at least neutral. She got things that I didn't even imagine existed: a contraption with something looking like a little bullhorn on top that she's supposed to attach to herself to collect milk, a grinder to make your own baby food, and all kinds of lotions just for babies. They had knit tiny, cockeyed sweaters and tie-dyed up those baby tee shirts that snap between the legs.

"I love the little duckie socks," said Slice, who had insisted on coming to the shower. "Adorbs!"

"Just *don't*," I said. Willow looked happy, glowing even, the way they say pregnant ladies are, and at that moment I'd imagined that things would be just fine. Everyone congratulated her and told her she'd be such a great mom, but I knew they were dying to get an inside story.

"I wonder what the baby will look like," they said to me, when what they meant was, *Won't you please, please, please just tell us who's been doing your sister?* I wouldn't mind knowing myself, but Willow was so going through it—I didn't dare.

A few people from high school had resurfaced, some of them looking just like I remembered, but other ones were such hot messes. This one guy who drove them to our house worked on the road crew, wearing an orange reflector vest. He had a tattoo on the side of his neck that sort of looked like an eye but might be a fish. He waited in his truck, the cab filling up with smoke and heavy-bass music.

Some of Willow's friends had finished school, but more had dropped out. A few went in the service, which was considered a wise move. The Army recruiting office sits right across the street from the high school in a strip of low buildings. It's in an old Baskin Robbins; you can still see the outline of the sign. They used to be good for those ice cream cakes they'd do in shapes, like a racecar or a bunny. Now it's where you go if you've shamed your parents so bad that you can't stick around town anymore. They take girls now, too. I heard that they'll give them free abortions for signing up. Still, it's a chance to begin again, to come up with a new version of yourself.

A couple of weeks into being a mom, this sadness clamped down on Willow. All she could do was sleep and sob. She had a rat nest going on in the back of her hair, so I had to remind her to get a bath and change her clothes, she was getting so ripe. Her miserable, the baby crabby, and our house shrinking more than I imagined it could. She wouldn't let me talk to anyone about her, afraid that Family Services would be in her face. I was worried about leaving her alone, but I couldn't sit there all day. When she wasn't for real asleep, she was pretending to be, hiding under the blankets. Passion yelped, and Willow just wouldn't hear her.

A couple of times, Willow jumped out of bed, pulled on her boots, and rushed out the door. "I can't take this anymore!" she'd say, but she never got far. Winter here, your tears will freeze right on your cheeks. She'd come back in ten minutes, blotchy and shaking. I'd boil two rounds on the kettle to add to our not-so-hot bath water, and she'd eventually go in there to thaw out in the tub. When we were little, this was how Mom would settle us down when we were crazy, with a good soak. It was a kind of absolution.

I wondered about Passion growing up here. As a kid, you only know what you see right in front of you, so you have no clue about what you haven't got. She'd grow up thinking that everyone lived in a trailer with their mood-swung mom and frazzled uncle, and about Willow and me people would say either we were lucky to have made it to adulthood or that we totally blew our chances. At first, Passion would never know that there were other ways to be a kid. Then one day she'd realize that breakfast-for-dinner wasn't just about fun, it was also about money.

143

Here's what I remember about being a kid: Mom sitting in the car, her back heaving, her forehead resting on the steering wheel. Her coming in all blotchy-faced, me wondering what I'd done to upset her. Using our grocery money to buy bottles of vitamin B-17, and Willow and I picking apricots around the valley after dark. There were plenty of places where the trees are right up next to the road. We didn't even have to go onto someone's land. Willow would just put me on her shoulders to grab the low-hangers. Mom said if you could reach it from the road, it was public. But still, she didn't want us to get shot, so we'd go when no one could see us.

Willow would get the flesh off the pits and make something of it. We had apricot everything: in the yogurt, as preserves, as jerky. We had no-brand corn flakes with it, or we'd freeze little chunks on toothpicks and pretend it was a fancy dessert. Occasionally it was peaches. Doesn't matter; you can eat and eat fruit and it's never going to fill you up. My job was to take the pits outside, smash them open with a hammer, and pry the kernel out with an old knife that had no serrations left on it. Mom had carried them in a little embroidered bag and nibbled at them all day. I tried one of those seeds once and it was horrible. It was like I'd imagine poison to be, all bitter and long-lasting in the back of your throat. Still, she treated them like gold nuggets.

She kept getting sicker and sicker. We'd had a pretty good life up until then, the three of us. Mom had a little studio in front of our trailer where she wove all day, and the tourists would come in and watch her. They'd buy these rugs she made, maybe seeing them as souvenirs, maybe as art. I guess it didn't matter because it allowed us our little triad of an existence. I helped her warp the loom, doing the bending-over part. There is a lot of math to it, people don't realize that, and I'd figure out the lengths with a carpenter's pencil on a grocery bag. I found those scraps of paper in a little stack in her studio after.

Mom had made the decision to be all holistic about it before we even knew she got sick, having explained it to her friends and to herself long before going so thin and ashen. *They are not putting that poison in me*, she'd said.

She had a duty to stay around here for you was what the social worker said. *You kids were left to fend for yourselves* was something the judge who made Willow my guardian said. We didn't argue. We just wanted to be left alone.

When Passion was about a month or so old, a lady called from an adoption place, said she was returning a message. They don't just call people looking for babies, she told me. I asked if maybe people at the hospital gave out the names of the moms they thought shouldn't have kids. It wasn't like that, she said. "Violation of privacy, unless there is a real question of danger." Like she was reading from a script. She wouldn't tell me much else, like when Willow had called, whether it was before or after Passion was born.

I shouldn't have said I was the uncle; I think she would have told me more if she thought Passion was my kid. Willow wasn't saying who and didn't seem slighted, yet there was no guy around. Every dude I ever saw her talk to over the age of fifteen was a suspect. Sometimes when I couldn't sleep, instead of counting sheep, I'd try to think of everybody she'd ever met. I sort of felt like this was all my fault. Not literally, of course.

We both fished around, but delicately. I got that the woman was calling from Texas but that the babies can end up anywhere. All I gave her was that I didn't know who the father was, and that Willow had a girl and the baby was healthy from what I could tell. When she asked me whether Willow had used drugs or alcohol, I didn't want to talk to her anymore. I was polite, though. I didn't want to eliminate any options, but her assuming we were dirtbags, that pissed me off. Still and all, I took her number.

"Before you go, may I ask," the lady said, "are you able to determine the race of the baby?" That's when I hung up. Passion living somewhere else sure would solve a whole lot of everything for us. I didn't feel anything like a parent, or even an uncle, to her. Maybe it takes a while. I remembered about bonding from the baby class, but they didn't explain it so well. They made it sound like magic.

I was anxious about them, of course I was. Willow was just so wretched all the time, but *somebody* had to go to work. We had bills from the midwife place and then for all the baby supplies, which, by the way, there is a ton of stuff they need for being so little. People always talked about how once they had kids, they were always owing. "Life as you know it is *over*," said this guy from the patrol, who's got a bundle of kids. Everyone laughed but him. And me.

I worried I'd fall asleep coming down the mountain at the end of the day, just nod off and slide into the ravine. Other times, I wished I would. Willow and Slice would be hugging each other at the funeral, both crying, her saying things like, "Ezra was working too hard, and all for me and the baby," instead of her practically ignoring me all the time or accusing me of eating all of the oatmeal.

Willow never left the house, took hermitting to a whole new level. She'd always have on my old sweats and a flannel and a blanket wrapped all around her, either sleeping or watching reruns of cop shows. None of those work or school friends of hers stopped by or even called. Her boots on the tray at the door never moved, caked with the same mud from the last time she took them off, maybe as far back as the firewood fight.

I used a personal day to drag the two of them to the baby check-up because I was thinking that if I didn't physically deliver them, Willow would try to cancel. At the free clinic everyone was sneezing and all whacked-out looking. You could smell the germs flying around.

When we got sick as kids, my mom took us to a lady who would make some medicine drinks that tasted like scrub. Leaves, twiggy things, and berries in a blender making something frothy and lumpy that we gagged down. She looked like a witch, but she was super nice and always remembered our ages and all types of random facts about us. When I fell off the roof and gashed my forehead, my mom did the mending herself. I got to pick out the thread, and the purple stitches held just as strong as any doctor's would have. Still, my mom told me that if I didn't tell, we'd get to have ice cream for dinner.

In the waiting room at the clinic was this girl who had been a few grades ahead of me. She was sitting there all twitchy, and I remembered how gorgeous I had always thought she was, me in seventh grade, terrified of girls, and her, a junior or thereabouts. She was perfection. Long flowy hair, goggle tan, and always a radically short skirt—even in the dead of winter—but with long underwear. That way you still remembered what her bare legs were like. She'd be hanging with one or another older guy from the hill, Jan or some guy like him, always a golden couple.

We were sitting there, this girl not recognizing me, and I thought, What the hell, I have a job and a truck. Dropped in all casual-like that I'm on the patrol. She said she was there for a prescription but didn't elaborate. Probably the free clinic isn't the absolute best place to meet the ladies, but here we were. So, we're yapping it up, me mostly, and I guess I said something funny, because she laughed, and HOLY CRAP, she's got those meth teeth, gone brown at the gums. Then I couldn't not look at them. They reminded me of a woodchuck. Not an easy thing to unsee.

Then Willow came out with the nurse, and everyone is smiling, and she hands Willow the bundle, which Willow holds out in front like she might get electrocuted, and the nurse is still smiling, and off we go.

We kept going like our lives were the same, sleeping and working our way through the season. A few more blizzards, an early thaw, then a refreeze. We kept watch on the hang fire up at the ridge, avalanche bombed, remembered other disasters.

One day up on the hill at break, when it was getting towards spring, Slice and I dropped off our radios for recharging and stuffed some lunch in our pockets to eat on the fly so we could catch a few quick runs. Sometimes a person needs to grab a half-hour that's not about dragging forty pounds of boundary netting or racing to wherever Jan was ordering at us to get to "like two hours ago." We weren't allowed to go around in our jackets when we were off duty, so rather than waste time changing, we'd just turn them inside out and let our pockets flap in the wind.

We headed for a tree run that has a sketchy drop-in that people tend to stay clear of, hoping it would be less skied-out. At the bottom, there is a little bowl where the run opens up nice and wide, but you're still surrounded by trees, like a handful of wilderness. It's an excellent spot to rest and have some quiet. It's also a good place to be if you need to cry all by yourself when you've just figured out what everybody else already knew, that you were about to become an orphan and that you might get shipped off to some strange family.

Slice was off peeing behind a tree that didn't hide him at all—which could be the reason they don't want us tooling around in our patrol jackets—when I heard a little wail. I hiked up to where it had come from, hoping it was only my imagination or the wind. Supposedly there were wolves' dens back that way.

There, in the well of a tree, the snow blown so deep that I couldn't see more than the top of his head, was a little kid with a bloody face. "Get a sled," I said to Slice, or rather, I screeched like a little girl. We shouldn't have left both of our radios, but they probably would have been dead by then anyhow. Slice took off for one of the yellow call boxes smattered around the slopes that connected to the medical center. They were from before cellphones, which freeze up anyway, and what with the curves of the mountain, the old-school, single-line phones were still the only real option.

The blood on the snow around the kid looked like one of those carnival splash paintings you make with a squirt bottle on a turntable. Bloody drool was coming out of the rectangle where his upper front teeth were supposed to be. I checked his pupils, and that he could wiggle his fingers and feel me tapping his feet. Not that I was a paramedic, but I knew some stuff from watching.

"I fell and lost my dad," the boy said. His tracks veered from the path everyone else had followed, making a straight shot for the tree. He had slipped right down into the pocket of soft snow. It's nearly impossible to climb out of a trench like that by yourself. Worse if it's deeper than you are tall.

He backed away when I tried to pull him up onto level ground. "It's okay," I said. "I'm like a policeman, but on snow," was all I could come up with. Sometimes kids went all stranger-danger on us, which makes it hard to find out if they've snapped something in two. I took off my jacket and showed him the logo on the back, then put it on right side out so that I'd look like less of a clown.

"Do you have the dogs?" he asked.

At first, I didn't know what he was talking about.

"The rescue dogs," the kid said.

"They're for if you're lost," I said. "You're not missing because here you are, with me." He looked at me like I was some typical adult who isn't really listening to him. He had on a day pass, which, while not having a name on it, did tell me that he was a visitor. Whoever got him the pass didn't put any ID on him at all—couldn't even be bothered to put a name on the helmet. Totally pissed me off. All the parents need to do is to write it out on the tape that we have sitting right there at the ticket counter and slap it on. Takes all of ten seconds.

"Who are you with?" I asked.

"Just us," he said. "Me and my dad. He was ahead

of me."

Nice. A father who races ahead of his kid and takes off. I got out of him that his name was Todd, he was nine, and they were on a "men's weekend." I wiped him down with my gaiter and some snow.

Jan snowmobiled towards us with the sled, with Slice riding the back seat like he was on a parade float. When the father finally turned up, right away we were wishing he'd stayed missing.

"Hey Todd, buddy, where'd you go?" he said. "I turned around and you were gone." All smiley. Totally not acting like his kid just smashed into a tree and was lucky to be standing. "Looks like you ruined that new jacket I got you."

"You'll need to come with," Jan said. "We need to get him checked out, do the incident report."

"He's fine. You're okay, right?" said the dad. "No need. Waste of time."

"I want to go inside," Todd said. "I'm cold. I need Mom." Slice got him a warming blanket from the sled.

The dad looked at his son like he was ashamed of him, like the kid should man up and just deal with it. He pulled out his wallet and said to Jan, "How about we just say it was a false alarm."

Todd looked ready to crumple. "My face hurts." He pulled back his puffed lip and touched the new gap with his tongue.

"Where the fuck are your teeth?" asked the dad. "We need them," he said, pointing to the splashes of blood. "And a dental surgeon."

"Around here? Yeah, right," I answered, which I hadn't meant to say out loud. The dad lunged at me, and right before the others took him down, I got a whiff of whiskey.

"You. Find them," he said, shoving his index finger at me. "Or you're all getting sued." Like we didn't hear *that* at least once a week. He signed a waiver when he bought their passes, and we all knew it. "I can't return the kid to that bitch without his teeth."

While Jan and I were busy being berated, Slice had hopped into the tree well and was yucking it up with Todd, having blocked the kid's view of his idiot father.

"I remember you now!" Slice said. "The pictures with the dogs!" The boy beamed.

"The day we met the dogs," said Todd. "You are there, in my picture! I have a new coat now. I didn't know if you'd know me. That one got too small." He looked down at his blood-spattered chest, the new jacket logoed up with a high-end brand that Willow could have easily had as a sponsor.

Slice right away distracted him with fabricated tales of his own wipeouts. "Oh, man, you should have seen it! Never found my poles!" High-fives galore. He handed the kid a mound of snow to numb up his lip. "This is how we do it on the fly," he said, and then carried him to the sled and strapped him in. Todd gave him his new jack-o-lantern smile. Somehow Slice knew just what the kid needed.

The dad hadn't even hugged his son. "I guess this is why your mom divorced me, huh?" The boy didn't look at him, and I thought: well, here's an iceberg I'll be glad to not see the rest of. Having no dad at all had to be better than having this one. No, that's a lie; both scenarios are horrible, just in different ways.

"Dad, they have a hospital here, and it's on stilts! In the snow!" Todd said. "And you get there in a snow-mobile instead of an ambulance!"

"Nice. A tree house with a witchdoctor and a box

of Band-Aids," the dad said. "Bunch of rubes."

I stayed behind to cover up the blood.

I still had my college brochures. In my favorite one, a tall guy walks between two girls. His backpack with the school emblem on it is slung on one shoulder, and he's talking to the shorter girl, blond, who grins up at him. On the opposite side of him was this other girl, watching them. The nicer, smarter best friend. I liked her curly, brown hair and glasses and her stack of books while her friend had none. A cliché, I know, but I'd had enough extraordinary. I kept the pamphlets good and buried. I didn't want to be setting Willow off.

Our landline got cut off, so I got her a pay-by phone. I don't think she ever talked to anyone because I never had to buy her any extra minutes. She slept whenever Passion did, which was a lot. When I asked her if she ought to get dressed, she said, "What, is the queen coming by?" like putting on daytime clothes is fancy. "That bitch at baby school who was talking about giving up Passion was right," Willow said. "I can't even figure out how to stop her from screaming." Meanwhile, I'm thinking, *You cry so much more than the baby does.*

I told Willow what I thought she needed to hear, that she was a good mom to me, and I wasn't even lying. And her only a kid at the time. I was rarely hungry, did well in school, got a job and wasn't in jail—all the opposite of what our old social worker had predicted. I still didn't tell Willow that the lady from the adoption place had called.

That little girl they found unconscious in the snow had seizures when she was in the hospital. The word was that she'd be in there for a while, having to do therapy and take a bunch of medicine, but that she could be okay, or something close to it. Eventually. She had frostnip on her face, which turns your skin white for a while. We all get that sooner or later. If it wasn't full-on frostbite, then she probably wasn't out there long. When I thought of her, I turned her into a young version of Willow, impatient to get back out on the hill, screaming at everyone to just let her alone.

Slice and I spent most of our work time hanging out, always riding the lifts together, mostly so that I didn't have to listen to the other patrollers go on about the same old crap, like which tourist lady they're banging and when they are leaving for Todos Santos in the spring. And what they are going to do when they win the lottery. Yeah, right. Keep me posted on that.

"So has any guy shown up?" Slice asked. He was so getting on my nerves about Passion's father. He was more worried about it than I was. Poor Slice.

I was finding late notices on bills I'd never seen, so I figured Willow had tossed them. She was good about taking Passion to her check-ups, especially when I dragged her there, but skipped her own. She cancelled the lady who came around to see that you know how to give a baby a bath and deal with the bellybutton business, even though she was free. Willow thought that somehow she would know that we had not yet paid the delivery bills and turn her in.

Sometimes I'd come home to an ammonia smell and Passion would be sopping wet and looking so sad. I doubt they went anywhere during the day. The baby doctor didn't like the diaper rash and liked even less that the back of Passion's head was getting flattish and no hair was peeking through that part of her skull. "She can't be on her back all day," she said. If I hadn't heard it whispered about me as a kid, I'd have said we were getting like trailer trash.

"You know there's a counselor at the clinic," I told Willow. A guy at work told me, said his sister was like Willow, post-partum. It's serious, more than just feeling bummed. Nobody's fault, just something that happens.

"I am NOT going to a fucking shrink!" Willow said. She slammed the door to her room, setting Passion off. She came back to the front of the house, plopped down in front of the TV like there wasn't a baby screaming her poor head off right around the corner. The trailer's walls are just ideas of walls; I didn't get how Willow could block her out like that. "Maybe Passion would be better, you know. With someone else," she said. "I suck at being a mom." And then, the husky wails and gulps of air. She went on for like an hour, but at least she was talking. Then she went on to us having no money and back to her being a lousy mom. More sobbing. "I do think about it, all the time," she said. "Giving Passion up. But don't tell anyone." She settled and hiccupped a bit, the blotches on her face mellowing. "Maybe I should," she said. This scene played out in one way or another what seemed like every day. Whatever I said would be the wrong thing.

Slice hung around our place all the time, more and more, until it was always. When I worked a later shift, I'd come home to him and Willow sitting on the couch watching *Judge Judy* and eating microwave popcorn with yeast. "Health food!" he'd say, holding up the bag like a trophy, spilling dusty kernels on Willow's head. He'd have Passion on his lap, which could only be good, since Willow hardly held her. His gym bag of I-don't-know-what had been sitting in the space between the fridge and the wall forever, clothes and plastic bags getting heaped on top, like a sideways-running crawl space full of his crap. Turns out his mom had this new guy she met at New Year's who had been led to believe that Slice was her little brother. She had him super young, so she's still totally in the game. Not *my* game, but she sure doesn't look like someone who has a kid old enough to kick out. Sometimes when you come upon her from a distance and she has her sunglasses on, you're like, "Well, *all right*," but then she gets closer and it's Slice's mom smiling back at you.

"You're turning into some family like they have on *Cops*, who'll end up out in the yard throwing cans at each other," Slice said.

"I think she's going to crack," I said.

"We need a plan." We were brainstorming, but with beers.

That's how I ended up digging around for the adoption lady's number, wanting to see what the options were. I'd heard that they had pictures of the families, and you could find out a lot about them and then pick, like shopping from a catalog. They would let you know how the kid was getting on, so you'd see how they were better at being parents. Willow could choose a family that was the way she wished we were, people who had figured out how to be adults. There were so many things that could go wrong with a kid, even if you were paying attention.

"We should become businessmen, we're so smart," Slice said.

I told the woman what I knew, which was a whole lot of nothing. Meanwhile, Slice fed me beers for fortitude. It felt good, this stepping up. She interrogated me about the father, making sure he wasn't going to appear and want Passion. I was ready to have Slice lie and say he was the dad, just to get her to relax already.

Then I'm thinking, hey, these people would be getting Passion, but they didn't have to go through all that Willow did, and we still have to deal with the piles of bills? That didn't seem right. So, I tell the woman this, but dancing around it, reminding her that we have no money and maybe she can sort us out, since these people would be getting a baby that had already been a lot of work and not at all cheap. She said she would call me right back, said she needed to check into something—excellent timing because I was overdue for a snack. Maybe she already knew a perfect family for Passion! Sure, I feel horrible about it now, and who wouldn't, but from there, it looked win-win. Willow could be happy again, and Passion gets a chance at a reasonable life.

When the adoption lady rang, Slice and I were tossing back a few while we looked under the furniture for quarters for the laundry. When she asked if I had an amount in mind, I just made stuff up, best-guessing what our bills were. I didn't add any extra on. Slice slid me another beer while she went on and on, asking me how we were, which was nice, again about the dad, and would Willow sign something saying the father was unknown. She was super-friendly.

I still hadn't told Willow, but I figured she'd be relieved. She was always saying things like Passion was going to hate her and grow up all screwy because of it. "Passion needs a better mom," she'd said, so many times.

The adoption woman made it sound so easy, like this happens all the time: someone other than the parent setting it all up. Looking back, it was a little strange that she never asked to talk to Willow.

For the first time in what felt like forever, I woke up with my jaw not feeling like I'd been chomping on rocks all night. Something of a hangover, though that was a fine trade-off for the dread that had been there every other morning.

"What did Willow think?" Slice asked as we loaded the lift. "Is she liking the plan?"

I had a rage of a headache, and he was looking like a human tumbleweed. We had two liters of Coke and a box of saltines from the gas station to help us get through the morning. Too decimated to manage long underwear, I'd pulled my ski pants on over my flannel pajama bottoms and they were all bunched up around my thighs. It felt like I was sitting on a pile of laundry, so I tried to shimmy both legs of my pants back down where they belonged.

"Quit swinging already," Slice said. "So, Willow. What's she think?"

I hadn't told her a thing, firstly because of my not having run our idea by her before talking to the Texas lady and secondly, truth, I didn't have the clearest memory of the conversation. "I didn't want to just dump this plan on her and then take off for work," I said. "You know how crazy she's been."

"Don't even," Slice said. "She's got loads to deal with. You can't imagine."

"And you can?" I said, "Who made you the expert?"

"My mom used to say all this about how her life ended when she got pregnant with me," he said. "I ruined everything. Not an awesome way to go about being a kid, dragging that around. As hard as it was for me, it had to be way more awful for my mom."

This was exactly why the adoption made sense. It wasn't just for me; it was also for Willow and Passion. That visiting nurse person who'd come to the house had gone on and on about bonding and how she was concerned that Willow wasn't doing it. All anyone told her was that they didn't think she was up to being a mom. The difference was I had the sense to keep it to myself. At least for a while, I did.

"You need to help me show her that this is a good solution," I said. "Tell her about the things your mom said." What terrified me was that Willow might not care one way or another.

When we unloaded at the top, Jan was waiting with a list a mile long of stuff he said was all super urgent. He's always all emergency 9-1-1, and then it's nothing. Budweiser was sponsoring an event, so we had to assume that everyone on the hill was wasted. The upside is that this also meant plenty of snowboard girls in bikini tops.

We got home to find Willow had dead-bolted herself into the house. Slice and I yelled and banged on the door. It's flimsy enough, but I didn't want to bust it down because I'd only have to fix it after. I pressed my nose to the place where the bottom of the warped door doesn't meet the jamb and sniffed for gas. Just in case. She opened the door and then bounced it off my head. I could hear that the door was hollow.

"You asshole," she said. "Mind your own business already." She was in a level-ten rage, the anger pouring out of her eye sockets. Slice scooted behind the truck.

"*Now* what's the matter?" I asked.

"I had a visit from the police today," she said. "And the district attorney."

I figured this had to be about all those bills she'd

been ignoring. "It'll be fine," I said. "My bonus comes in in like two weeks. We can pay everything off just fine."

"You dope. They were looking for you. Not me."

"Oh. Wait, what?"

"Any chance you tried to *sell my baby*?" Willow said.

Here would have been an awesome time for Slice to step in and defend me, but he just went on crouching out of view. At first, he was laughing, because he didn't have the sense to be terrified. That adoption lady had been too nice to not have been up to something. Her with all the *y'all* and *honey* and *you poor dears*. She was good.

I told Willow it's all a misunderstanding, but she was already thrashing around in the kitchen. Passion was screeching, like she does, and then Willow was dragging my stuff out of my room and throwing it outside. My cowboys and Indians sleeping bag that I unzip and use flat like a comforter, the one I've had from before I can remember, tossed into a mud puddle. The liquid seeped through and made a giant, brown-edged wet spot, the water line spreading towards the zipper. When the pictures on it sunk under the water, my lungs felt like an accordion being pushed shut.

"Let me explain," I said, but she had already gone back inside. Our driveway had become the go-to place for big-ass temper tantrums.

Slice peeked out of his hiding place. "Think she's mad?" he said, like he's funny. "I'll talk to her." Yeah, you do that, Slice. He went inside for so long that I finally had to go take a leak by the side of the house, like some kind of a hobo. A neighbor was cooking up something beefy with red sauce. It smelled like our high school lunchroom, but I still wanted some. Willow was yelling, then crying, then they were both whispering, then no one's talking and Passion went quiet. So, either everyone was dead, or Slice worked some kind of miracle.

After a bit, he brought me a cheese and pickle sandwich, and we sat on the stoop in the dark. It was nice, just being there, the coyotes yipping to each other, us not having to say anything about the stupidity of the plan and what do we do now. In the dark like that, we could have been ten-year-olds again, our sadness focused on the immediate fact of the end of the season coming, rather than on how our lives were turning out.

Slice sat bolt upright like a current went through him. "How about this," he said. "I'll stay with Willow and Passion, and you go. Move away." But he said this as if he hadn't just in the moment thought this up. More like he'd been stewing on this for a while, waiting for the right chance to drop it on me.

"I can't just leave her," I said. "She's such a mess."

"Guess what," he said. "We're *all* a mess."

Soon enough, two policemen came back with a warrant for trying to sell a baby over state lines. That lady had gotten a cop to listen in when she called back. They recorded it and played it for the D.A. and the judge, who said they could come on over to our house and pick me up.

I could tell by the way that they looked around our place that this visit wasn't going to be good. It was beer cans, ski magazines, and dirty clothes all over the place. We had moved into a shack without ever going anywhere. Willow and Passion were passed out in the back, exhausted from all the wailing. The cops didn't even bother to check if there was a baby to begin with, they were so stoked to be handcuffing me. They read me my rights, which were exactly the way they say them on TV: you have a right to remain silent, stuff you say can and will be used against you, and all that. You'd have thought I was on a wanted flyer in the post office, with a big fat reward, they were so into it. They dragged me in right then and there, in the middle of the night.

By the time we got to the station, they had nowhere to put me. Since I'm a minor, they couldn't toss me into the regular part where they leave people to dry out, and juvie was closed-up for the night. A cop had to sit with me until court opened. All night it was the two of us in his office, with him drinking coffee from a mug from the Salt Lake City Winter Games, the Olympic circles worn off by his fat fingers. He was supposed to clamp me to a chair, but I embarrassed him out of it when I told him I had gone to school with his kid, who we both knew was even more of a train-wreck than Willow and me combined. We played hangman on the back of a flyer for a pancake breakfast that was going on the next weekend for that little girl who was found in the snow. I wished I'd been able to say that I was the one who'd found her, to prove that I wasn't a total loser. When trampling him in hangman and then tic-tac-toe got boring, I slumped in a corner on the floor and slept.

At the arraignment, where they make you stand there and listen to what they think you've done without any chance to give your side, I was assigned one of those free lawyers. This guy looked about as old as me, but dopier.

"Hey man, haven't I seen you up on the hill?" he said, trying to relate. The first thing he told me was that the good news was my age, that if I plead out (which meant admitting I would try to sell a baby!), it wouldn't go on my record. Before he had even heard my version.

Then he played that tape. That adoption lady and me. Wasted, wasted me.

I had to get Willow to put up the deed for the trailer so I could get out. A new social worker turned up wanting a restraining order to keep me from Passion. Like I was going to grab her and stick her on eBay. She said things like *unscrupulous* and *deviant* without ever having met me.

The free lawyer wasn't so useless after all. "You do *not* want this to go to trial. Take the plea," he said. "Call those colleges and tell them you're coming. Do it before you are in the system, on your application that's already there, where you said you had never been arrested. Whoever bites first, that's where you're going." So maybe I hadn't blown my chances. "This way, at sentencing we can say you have a plan for your future," he said. "The D.A. will be glad to know you're leaving town. Maybe even buy you the bus ticket." He wanted me to round up some people who could vouch for me. I dreaded trying to explain all this to Jan and my counselor from the high school: *I accidentally tried to sell my niece, but not really, I was just drunk.* No one wants to hear that.

Willow came to court and swore I wasn't dangerous or crazy, just like my lawyer told her. She told the judge that she was having a hard time and that this was all a misunderstanding, so would he please let me come home. She didn't have to fake the crying. Slice had his arm on her shoulder the whole time, letting her wipe her nose on the hem of his shirt. The two of them came off so respectable, and me as a total whack.

We never got to the part where Willow would say that when I was little, I had no parent around and that's why I made bad choices.

The judge let me go with conditions. Probably the juvenile hall was full or something. Slice put Willow and Passion in his car to drive from the courthouse, since I wasn't allowed to take her anywhere. Neither of them looked at me in the parking lot. Part of me was so mad at Slice, who was an instigator, yet acting like this was news to him. I also was thankful that he was handling Willow, which sure was more than I had managed.

I couldn't go up on the hill anymore because it's out of range for my "new jewelry," so said the cop who clamped the monitor on my ankle. I don't think I could have gotten a boot on over the thing anyhow. And since I wasn't eighteen, I couldn't even apply to go on road crew with Tattoo-neck. Even the Army recruiters would have had to turn me down. Not that it would be even close to what I was making, but I called the café where I used to work, to see if they'd take me back, hoping my old boss hadn't heard or didn't care. I was still someone who could count change and would remember to show up.

The next day was a bluebird morning, after a sweet foot of powder fell overnight. It hurt my heart to look outside. Willow and Slice had me watch Passion, which was cool, because they showed that they knew I wasn't the devil. Seriously, where was I going to go, anyhow? I assumed they were off running errands, but it turned out that Slice took Willow skiing. She was so chirpy when they got back, that I should have figured it wasn't about a run to Big Lots. I wouldn't have even known they'd gone up but for her boots drying in the kitchen next to his.

"I want to be here, get it? There's nothing waiting for me somewhere else," Slice said, still going on about me leaving town and him staying. "I never wanted to split. That was all you." It felt too easy, for me to just walk away and suddenly he's basically a parent.

That night, when Passion was so tired that she cried herself into a red-hot ball of misery, Slice went right to her, took her for a snuggle on the couch. While *Jeopardy* was on, Slice asked Passion's opinion on his guesses, which were rarely correct. She wrapped her chubby hand around his index finger. Even after finally going to sleep, she wouldn't let go. Passion *had* bonded to someone; it just wasn't Willow. Or me.

I called the colleges that had let me in and found two that would still give me scholarships. Not my top picks, but decent-enough schools, far away from here, one in a city and one not. I had never in my life ridden in a subway.

I took the plea.

"Good thing you pulled this stunt while you were still underage, huh?" said the lawyer, like a bighead. He made leaving town a condition of the agreement, marketing it to the D.A. as something safer for Willow and Passion. "Reckless endangerment," which, as he said, reads from afar like I was just out on a bender punching people or stealing road signs. I told myself that if I left and went to college, I could get a better job and that it would come back to Willow. Still, it felt like running.

I sweat through the same waking dream over and over:

Passion as a toddler, learning to ski. Her wild blonde hair sticks out from underneath a pink helmet. Slice is behind her, braking, holding her back with a harness. Her skis, just over two feet long, are making the shape of a slice of pizza, pointed together at the tips, her inside edges down. Still too little to use poles, her arms shoot out to the side like a scarecrow's. She keeps looking back to Slice, which I worry will make her cross her tips and fall. But she doesn't. "Faster! Faster!" she says, as the traffic on the bunny hill stops to watch them pass.

When I said I was leaving, Willow barely took her eyes off the TV. I wish she'd screamed or thrown a plate at my head or at least slung a few curses. I excused my way around the move, blaming it on the judge, my attorney, everyone but myself. She never brought up the fact that she had not abandoned me, but it was there, hanging between us like dust motes. I owed her everything, and we both knew it.

"We can use the space," Willow said. "The sooner you get your crap out of here, the better." She went into the back, slammed the door, leaving Passion and Slice with their game show and me wondering whether she was muffling her crying with a pillow or if she was already making plans for my room.

I left behind all my stuff that had to do with snow. My fat powder-day skis, the beater pair for when the cover was thin, a crazy-long pair from the eighties that were just funny to have around, and dinged-up slalom ones with ruined edges that Jan handed down to me for hard pack. Most of my clothes: base layers, bulky ski pants, and subzero jackets I'd never need where I was going, I jammed into giant plastic bins. I was going to do a yard sale, but Slice talked me out of it.

"Off season, you'll get like nothing for this gear," he said. "I'll hold onto it for you. For when you come back."

There was little left for me to take. I packed up in a couple of hours. When I pulled down a faded poster of Chamonix, the holes that the tacks left in the particleboard were like old wounds. I measured my childhood by the difference in color between what was under the poster and the rest of the wall.

Perhaps Willow would eventually love Slice back, but maybe not. I wasn't sure that she had it in her anymore. Being around the two of them would have to be enough for him. He'd stick around and be there for Passion when Willow couldn't. He'd dig in and refuse to leave, through the one or three or seven years or whatever it took for Willow to wise the hell up.

When I pulled out of the drive, the tires of my unweighted truck spun mud back at the trailer. There were good odds that I'd never return. It felt like a beginning and a broken heart, all at the same time. I dreaded seeing the contrast between the only place I'd ever known and the rest of the world.

ACKNOWLEDGEMENTS

A world of gratitude to the publishers at EastOver Press: Denton Loving, Keith Pilapil Lesmeister, Kelly March, and Walter M. Robinson. Thanks for supporting my stories in particular, and short-form writing in general. Thanks to my editor, Anna Schachner, for your acumen, grace, and flexibility.

Thanks to the following journals for publishing, some in different versions, stories from this collection: *Harpur Palate, Entropy, Tahoma Literary Review, Jabberwock Review, Jet Fuel Review,* and *Prick of the Spindle.*

I owe much to the people and institutions who have expanded, supported, and enriched my writing life: Bennington Writing Seminars; Alda Sigurðardóttir and the Gullkistan Artists Residency in Laurgavatn, Iceland; Prospect Street Writers House; Anji Brenner and the Mill Valley, California Public Library; Peg Alford Pursell and Why There Are Words; Tin House; SOMOS (Taos, New Mexico); Sewanee Writers' Conference; Bread Loaf Writers' Conference; Vermont College of Fine Arts; and the

Tomales Bay Workshops. I have been truly fortunate to have met such an array of writers and bibliophiles; in fact, there are too many to list. Know that all of you are a part of this book.

I want to thank the following for spending time with these stories, some in earlier drafts: Peter Trachtenberg, David Gates, Amy Hempel, Charles Baxter, Ron Carlson, Lidia Yuknavitch, Jill McCorkle, Steve Yarbrough, Tomás Morín, Ellen Lesser, Hasanthika Sirisena, Robert Boswell, and Bret Anthony Johnston. I appreciate your honest critique as well as the encouragement.

To my writer friends, including but not limited to: Joanne Nelson, Cathy Maclin, Jean-Marie Saporito, Kelly Sather, V Hansmann, Jia Oak Baker, Lisa Krueger, Jan Smith, Barrett Warner, C. Rizleris, Lee Prescott, and Kelly Alsup. I am so grateful for your comradery, support, candor, and friendship.

Thank you to my students for your enthusiasm, your openness to experimentation, your questions, and your amazing words. Onward!

I'd be remiss in not mentioning the villages of Arroyo Seco and Taos Ski Valley, New Mexico, where these stories were born. Kudos to lifties everywhere for the grueling work they do, and to the Taos Ski Valley Ski Patrol, particularly the patrollers who answered my many avalanche questions.

Lastly and most importantly—all the love in the world to my family. Thanks to my mother, Ursula, for the encouragement, close reading, and attention to storm warnings.

To my husband, Dan, and our daughter, Leyton, thank you for your support, love, and time—as well as for the snow days. This one's for you.

ABOUT THE AUTHOR

LINDA MICHEL-CASSIDY lived for 15 years in voluntary exile in rural Northern New Mexico. She is a writer, critic, teacher, editor, and visual artist. She is a senior book reviews editor at *Tupelo Quarterly*, where she also contributes criticism, and for several years, was a contributing editor at *Entropy Magazine*. She holds an MFA in fiction from the Bennington Writing Seminars, and another, in visual arts, from the California College of the Arts. She was a cross-disciplinary resident at Gullkistan in Laugarvatn, Iceland, and a visual arts resident at Brazier's Park in Ipsden, England. Michel-Cassidy is a mediocre skier and has recently taken up open-water swimming. She currently lives between Arroyo Seco, New Mexico, and a houseboat in Sausalito, California.